AF378431

For _Alice_

Happy New Year! 2020
Lots of love

Auntie Susan
& Minos xxx

THE AMAZING ADVENTURES OF THE MALEKIDI MOGGIES

by **Valerie Knight** with illustrations by **Katie Sabry**

© 2019 Valerie Knight (Text) - Katie Sabry (Illustrations)

Design and layout: Kyriaki Sofocleous (Not So Big Fish Productions)
Photography of Illustrations: Vassos Stylianou
Printed by: H. Loizides Printers & Lithographers

Mikrokyklos
B o o k s

The publishing imprint of
K.M. KYRIAKOU FULLPAGE BOOKSHOPS LTD
29, Panathinaion Str., 3031 Limassol, Cyprus

Mailing Address:
P.O.Box 50806, 3610 Limassol, Cyprus
email: mikrokyklos@kfbooks.com
Tel. +35725343442   +35799414842
Fax +35725342195

ISBN 978-9925-7568-0-3

For Leon.
In memory of my parents.
K.S.

For all the countless moggies
who have brightened my life –
especially Zoe and Chloe.
And in memory of Amy.
V.K.

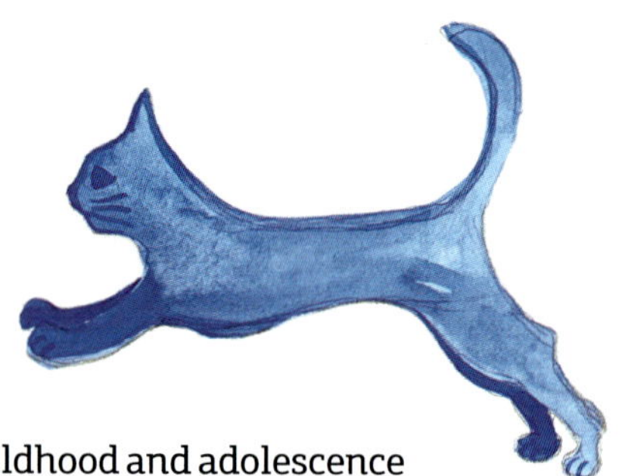

Valerie Knight's entire life has been nomadic – childhood and adolescence in Iraq, Iran and Libya (when they were still kingdoms), 12 years in various parts of Australia, and a couple of years each in Amsterdam and Italy, with intermittent periods in London, Dorset and Devon. Through all the years of moving around, two great loves remained constant: books and cats. She spent several years working as a freelance copy editor in the UK and Australia and has had articles published in magazines as diverse as *The Oldie* and *Kindred Spirit*. Her short stories have appeared in a number of anthologies, including Ginninderra Press (Australia) and Sentinel (UK). In 2014 she published her first novel *The Elusive Soulmate*. She first met Katie Sabry and the real-life Malekidi Moggies shortly after she arrived in Cyprus in 2010 and this book is the result of a happy collaboration between writer and illustrator. After all the decades of moving around the planet, Valerie now feels relatively settled in Limassol where she shares her seaside flat with a one-eyed cat called Chloe.

Katie Sabry has been an artist for as long as she can remember, growing up mostly in Kyrenia, on the north coast of Cyprus, surrounded by cats, books, wonderful untouched landscapes, and pristine beaches. She feels that all this, coupled with the fact that both her parents were artists, provided the perfect foundation for a fruitful imagination and love of the natural world. Katie lived, worked and studied in England, Italy and Germany, before settling in Limassol in 1987 and opening her first studio that same year. She moved to Number 9 Malekidi Street in 1994, where she has lived and worked as an artist ever since. Katie also designs and makes mosaics, has been a stained glass designer and maker, a silver service waitress, and an artist's life model. Her first love has always been observing and painting pictures of Cyprus landscapes, trees, cats and the sea. The magic carpet is still somewhere in Number 9, and who knows what other mysteries await in Katie's house and magical garden...?

CONTENTS

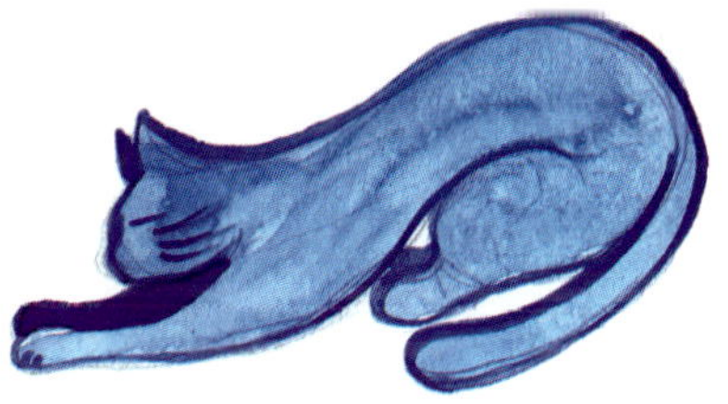

1

LET'S MEET THE MALEKIDI MOGGIES

Once upon a time there were four friendly moggies who lived together in the seaside town of Limassol on the sunny island of Cyprus.

Their names were Loulou, Sylvester, Hissie and Winnie and they shared their home with a kind-hearted snuzzle called Katie. ('Snuzzle' is cat-speak for 'human'. Man or woman, boy or girl, as far as cats are concerned they are all snuzzles.)

Katie had a lovely magical house right in the middle of the town but it was our four moggy-friends who turned that house into a home. You probably already know that's what cats do, they turn houses into homes, that's their job.

Loulou was a very wise and dignified elderly gentleman with a magnificent shiny black coat and green eyes that looked deep deep into the very heart of you and understood all your biggest secrets and all your biggest worries and made you feel safe. Loulou hadn't *always* been wise. He had grown that way because every time he made a mistake when he was growing up he sat quietly with his eyes closed and his paws together and made a strong promise not to make the same mistake again. That's what makes you wise – learning from your mistakes until one day, when you're old, you discover you have stopped making mistakes in the first place. Now, as you read about our four friends' amazing and sometimes dangerous adventures, you will understand what a very good thing it was that one of them was so wise, because, when someone is wise, they can stop you from making a really stupid mistake and that's very important when you're going on a Big Adventure.

Sylvester was a little old lady-cat and that might surprise you because Sylvester is a boy's name. But the thing is that Sylvester was so extremely courageous and eager to Have A Go that she really had a boy's heart beating in her old lady's chest. We all know that girls can be as brave as lions but boys can be much more reckless and this is how Sylvester had been even when she was a tiny kitten – a proper tomboy, never happier than when she was getting into scrapes. Her parents would sigh and say to each other, 'She's so pretty with her black coat and little feet and pink nose but all she wants

to do all day is climb up trees so she can jump on somebody and give them a fright. She's so like a boy we'd better give her a boy's name.' And so she became Sylvester. And it's good to have someone like that on your Big Adventures, too, because she looks so sweet and dainty that bad cats don't take any notice of her and then she can give them a big surprise – and a big wallop.

Hissie was also a lady-cat but a little younger than Sylvester and very different. Hissie was anxious and nervous about *everything*, from loud noises to getting a bit of dust on her luxurious pearl-grey coat. Her catch-phrase was 'Oh, do you think that's a good idea? – it might be dangerous or it might make us late for tea or... or... or...' But everybody loved Hissie because she was like everyone's favourite Auntie and this is

also a good thing when you're going on a Big Adventure. It's good for you to have someone a little anxious you have to care for because it keeps you kind. It's very easy to forget to be kind when you're having a Big Adventure.

And now we come to Winnie. And what can we say about Winnie? Winnie was an extremely handsome young man with more energy than was really good for him. He had long legs which meant he could run

very fast and jump very high so he could get out
of scrapes as easily as he could get into them.
He thought life and the whole world had been
created just for his personal amusement.
He was so full of the joys of spring that,
even when he was being impossibly
naughty and keeping everyone awake
when they wanted a nice snooze, nobody
could be angry with him for long. He had
such a funny long nose and could pull such
funny faces that, even when you wanted to be
cross, you couldn't help laughing. And it's also
very good indeed to have someone like Winnie
when you're going on Big Adventures because
he can keep everyone's spirits up and also
isn't afraid of rushing into danger at a moment's
notice. In fact, he loves it.

So now you've met our four feline adventurers
('feline' is people-speak for any kind of cat, big or
small, wild or tame). And later on, when news of their
Amazing Adventures spread and began to be written
down in books like this one, the names of Loulou, Sylvester, Hissie and Winnie became
famous all over the world, from Bristol to Billygazonkaland (which is a very long way
away). And every kitten on the planet wanted to be just like them and would beg
their parents to tell them bedtime stories about where they had been and the battles
they had fought – and about their Miraculous Magical Carpet, which you'll hear more
about in just a little while.

The house where our heroes and heroines lived was Number 9 Malekidi Street
in Limassol and it was a very special place. Limassol is a busy, bustling town and
when you walked past Number 9 Malekidi Street, all you could see was a front door,
just like any other front door. Nothing very interesting about *that*. But if you were
lucky enough to be invited inside, well, then it was a very different story. The house
was long and thin and it went back a long, long way, with doors opening out on
either side. There were beautiful black and white tiles on the floors, and white walls
covered with big colourful paintings which made you think of other worlds. And,
best of all, just when you least expected it, there in front of you was a garden that
made you think you had stepped into Paradise!

And because the garden was surrounded by high walls, nobody passing the house would ever guess this garden existed. It was a complete secret from the outside world – just the sort of place for happy cats to live in and plan Adventures. And just the sort of place for a kind-hearted snuzzle like Katie to live, because Katie was an artist who spent her days mixing beautiful colours and turning them into paintings for people to put on their own walls at home so they, too, could have a bit of Malekidi Magic all for themselves.

And Katie loved flowers and trees and they loved her back so everything in the garden grew and grew. There were big shady trees, perfect for cats to climb, and flowering bushes for them to hide in, and pots of scented herbs for them to sniff at. And in summer the garden was filled with a strange buzzing music which came from the big fat beetles known as cicadas (or *ziziros* in Greek which is the language of Cyprus). It sounded like a gigantic orchestra and took a bit of getting used to but the cats and Katie liked it. It made them smile and feel a little bit lazy and dreamy which is a very nice way to feel.

And there were lizards and skinks and emerald-green praying mantises, all going about their business in the pots and the shrubs and trying not to get pounced on by Winnie when he was feeling naughty or bored.

So this was the fabulous secret world where Loulou, Sylvester, Hissie and Winnie lived their happy lives and they often climbed right up, up, up on to the roof of Katie's house where they were completely safe from any cars or dogs in the street below and where they could stretch out and sniff the breeze and dream their dreams.

Sometimes Loulou would tell them stories about the Old Days, or Sylvester would describe some of her narrow escapes when she was young, or Hissie would sing soothing songs to them, because that made her stop being anxious.

And what of wild young Winnie? What was *he* thinking about as he sprawled on the roof listening to the older ones' songs and stories? He was thinking that it was all very well living in such a lovely place with plenty of food and lots of lizards to chase and kind friends who loved him even when he was naughty, but there must be *Something More...* Surely, just over there, over the rooftops and out towards the sparkling Mediterranean Sea, there must be the possibility of bigger Adventures than Loulou or Hissie or Sylvester had ever had before...

'I know!' he said to himself. 'If I wish very hard, I'm *sure* I can make something amazing happen!'

And as you're about to find out, he was right...

A garden that made you think you had
stepped into Paradise!

WINNIE'S MAGICAL DISCOVERY

It was a beautiful afternoon in May and Winnie was bored. Why did the grown-ups *always* want to sleep after lunch? Loulou, Hissie and Sylvester were all drowsing up on the roof and weren't the least bit interested in Winnie's shenanigans.

He had tried everything he could think of to get their attention: he had hung by one paw from the gutter and then he had raced up the highest tree and pretended to be stuck at the top. He had even fallen from the roof accidentally on purpose and pretended to hurt his foot. He had limped around the garden (often forgetting which foot he was meant to be limping on) and kept on looking up at the roof with big sad eyes and pitiful '*meeeeeows*' but even this didn't get the others' attention. They had got so used to his antics that they had stopped taking him seriously and so they just burrowed their noses back under their paws and went on snoozing.

Winnie sighed and then he yawned and then he decided he was the most unfortunate boy-cat in the whole of Limassol and so he let out a mighty groan. But, then, wait a minute...! Had he spotted something out of the corner of his eye? Yes! There was a sudden movement beside the lavender bush and Winnie instantly knew what it

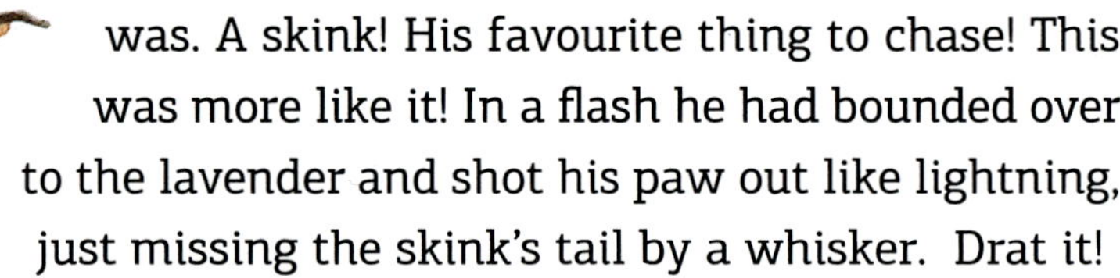

was. A skink! His favourite thing to chase! This was more like it! In a flash he had bounded over to the lavender and shot his paw out like lightning, just missing the skink's tail by a whisker. Drat it! The skink rushed off to the safety of a clump of rosemary and sat very still for several minutes until he was certain that Winnie had forgotten all about him. Then he slid out *very very slowly*, intending to run up the trunk of the lemon tree. Big mistake! Winnie hadn't forgotten him at all! He was off again, wild and excited and full of bounce. This was fun! The chase was on and life was worth living again! Winnie felt energy rushing up and down his long legs and out to the very tips of his whiskers. He didn't really want to *catch* the skink – at least, not too soon – what he really wanted was a jolly good gallop about.

Realising he couldn't make it safely to the tree because he would have to run across some open ground, Slinky Skinky made a dash for the house. The back door was open as usual and he felt sure he would be able to find some safe place to hide inside.

This plan suited Winnie very well too and he was perfectly happy to let the skink get safely over the threshold and into the house because it was always more fun to charge about indoors, rather than out in the garden. Indoors you could leap over tables and slide under chairs and squeeze behind cupboards, knocking things over in the process so there were some glorious crashing and smashing noises as well.

And it was this decision – to let the skink get safely indoors – which led to the biggest and most exciting discovery of Winnie's whole life...

The skink scuttled inside and then zoomed across the kitchen floor and over the black and white tiles into the hall where Katie had some beautiful pieces of sculpture on the floor and colourful paintings on the walls. But it wasn't the sculptures or the paintings that Skinky was interested in. No! – with his sharp little eyes he had spotted the perfect hiding place. There, rolled up in the corner, was an old rug and, before Winnie could even *think* about pouncing, the skink had run right inside the middle of that rolled-up rug and was as safe as could be. He squatted in the dark getting his breath back and congratulating himself on his quick thinking. He knew that the tiny opening was far too small and awkward for Winnie's paws and claws to reach. Phew! Everything was OK.

Now, even though we all know that Winnie is a very impatient young man-cat, he decided to settle down beside the rug in the hope that Skinky would come out and make a run for it. He was prepared to wait a very long time if necessary (well, five minutes, anyway...) He sat quietly at the tiny entrance to the skink's hiding place, his nose on his paws and his whiskers all atwitch. It looked as if his eyes were closed but they weren't really, they were open just enough to see what was going on.

Or so he *thought*...

Because, all of a sudden, something bopped him on the nose, really *hard*! 'Ouch! What was *that*?' Winnie jumped up, rubbing his nose with his paw, and looked all around but there was nothing to be seen. This was most puzzling. He didn't know what to make of it at all. He knew he couldn't have imagined it. After all, his nose was stinging – just like the time he had brushed up against that clump of nettles.

He sat down with his back to the rug for a moment and decided to have a little think when, *Wallop*! something bopped him on the bum! He whirled around just in time to see the most extraordinary sight. The rug itself had lifted up its tassels and was getting ready for a bit of fisticuffs!

Winnie couldn't believe his eyes. I mean, how many times have *you* been walloped on the bum by the tassels on a rug? It just doesn't happen, does it? But it *had* happened and Winnie took a great leap backwards. The rug looked perfectly normal again, all rolled up with the skink safely tucked away inside but as soon as Winnie began to creep towards it again, up came the tassels and gave a little warning shake.

This was even more exciting than chasing a skink! – but it was also a tiny bit scary. He had never even heard about such a thing before. Skinks, yes... Dogs, yes... But being told off by a *carpet*? Hmmm...

Winnie put his head on one side for a moment and as he pondered the situation his already long face looked longer than ever. That always happened when he was thinking about Something Serious. And, yes, he decided, this was definitely Something Serious. This was something he absolutely had to tell Loulou about...

Winnie bounded back across the black and white tiles and out into the garden.

Then he sprang up the trunk of the big tree and leapt from its topmost branch on to the flat roof where the others were stretched out in the warm sunshine. He rushed across to where Loulou was snoozing, tapped him on the shoulder with his paw and then bent down and whispered loudly in the old black cat's ear:

'Loulou! Wake up! You've got to listen to me! I've been bopped on the bum by a rolled-up carpet! Honest! And, look, it bopped me on the nose too –*Look!*'

Winnie was so used to not being believed when he came out with one of his stories that he fully expected to have to beg the others to listen to him.

So he was most surprised to see that Loulou was looking at him very intently and that Hissie and Sylvester had sat up and were whispering together. Nobody had told him to shut up. Nobody had accused him of making up tall stories. This was *most* unusual.

'Where did this happen and what were you doing at the time?' Loulou enquired after a long pause. He sounded Extremely Serious and Winnie instinctively knew he must be on his best behaviour.

'I was in the hall and I was chasing a skink,' he replied truthfully. 'And the skink ran inside that old rolled-up rug and I was waiting for it to come out again so I could chase it and maybe catch the end of its tail...'

'Aaaaah!' Loulou growled in an even more serious voice than before. 'You were chasing a skink for fun... You were giving him a big fright just so you could have a big laugh, was that it?'

'Well, yes,' Winnie admitted, 'but I didn't want to hurt him, not really, I just wanted a game...'

Loulou turned away from Winnie for a moment and faced the two ladies:

'I think it's time we told him, don't you?'

Hissie and Sylvester nodded gravely and Winnie suddenly discovered he was shaking with excitement:

'Tell me what? he exclaimed, jumping about on his gangly legs. 'Tell me *what*?! You all know something! You've got a secret from me, haven't you? Well, *haven't you*?!'

By way of reply, Loulou slowly stood up and had a massive stretch and a huge yawn. He didn't normally like being woken from his siesta but this was different, this was important – *really* important.

Silently the wise old moggy led the way back down from the roof and into the house, with Hissie, Winnie and Sylvester following him in a little procession.

Winnie could hardly contain himself. Why were they all so quiet? What had Sylvester and Hissie been whispering about? And, most important of all, why had Loulou immediately believed him? It was all very odd – and very exciting – to a young rascal.

At last they reached the hall and Loulou beckoned for them all to sit down beside the rolled-up rug. The hall was cool and dark because it was shaded from the daylight by big shutters and this added to the air of mystery and magic. Everything in the hall was just as it had always been and yet, at the same time, everything seemed different and Winnie felt as if he were standing on the very edge of the world.

Then Loulou closed his eyes and placed his right forepaw very gently and reverently upon the rolled-up rug. He took a deep breath and sat up very straight and tall and then he did something Winnie had never seen or heard Loulou do before – he started to sing. He sang quietly and in a deep voice that seemed to echo from thousands and thousands of years ago so that even lively long-legged Winnie became very quiet and still and respectful.

And this is what Loulou sang:
'Oh magic carpet so wise and old
Tales of your courage will soon be told –
Of your hues so bright and rich and bold
And of every stitch with its heart of gold...'
As the last notes of the song died away, a great sense of peace descended on the little gathering and finally Loulou smiled and spoke:

'You can all open your eyes now because it's finally time for me to recount the wondrous tale of this very special rug,' he said, looking at each of the others in turn before carrying on: 'Of course, Hissie and Sylvester, you already know most of it but for you, Winnie, it will be completely new and will change your life forever.'

Winnie's eyes were on stalks now and were as big as saucers. Change his life? Forever? Wow! This sounded *good*!

'This is no ordinary rug,' Loulou said. 'It has magical powers and an extraordinary history:

'It was first made by a good, kind wizard called Shentoro in the high mountains of Zennadon more than a hundred years ago. This wizard, together with his equally famous cat, the noble Derrashah, was known all over the world for his exquisite magic carpets which could fly high above the earth in complete silence and at tremendous speed (although the flight was always so calm and smooth that you hardly knew you were flying at all). He was very careful about who bought his carpets because he had one special rule which could never be broken: his carpets could be used only for Good.

'But one day, when Shentoro and Derrashah were away from home, attending a wizards' convention on a distant planet, a cruel and greedy robber broke into the wizard's secret storehouse and stole this very rug. This robber had committed hundreds of robberies over the years and in the process he had killed a lot of snuzzles – and moggies too. He was the very last creature in the world Shentoro would have allowed to buy one of his extra-special carpets.

'How the robber laughed when he sneaked out of the secret storehouse with the rug rolled under his arm. "He can't be much of a wizard," he chuckled. "It was so easy to pinch this beautiful carpet! Oh, how much easier my work will be now! What a fine time we shall have together, me and my miraculous magic carpet!" And he chortled again and slobbered lots of green spit all down his bristly chin.

'But, as you've probably guessed,' Loulou went on, looking round at his spellbound audience, 'Shentoro was no fool. True, the robber had stolen the rug but he was in for a nasty shock!

'Because the carpet refused to budge! It would forever and forever remain under the wizard's spell of kindness and could never be used for anything but Good. And so it didn't matter what the grumpy robber did. It didn't matter how often he jumped up and down or how loudly he bellowed or how much he threatened and swore, the carpet wouldn't do anything he demanded, not a single sausage.

'The robber got angrier and angrier until, finally, he was in such a rage that he picked up the disobedient rug and tried to rip it in two with his bare hands. He pulled and he pulled and he got it between his big yellow teeth and he almost managed to tear it in half. Almost, but not quite... The rug just managed to hold itself together by a few inches in the middle. It looked very sorry for itself but, most importantly, it hadn't been destroyed.

'By this time the robber was getting bored with his attack on the rug and so he slung it over his massive shoulder, marched out of his robber's cave and chucked it into a hedge with a bad-tempered growl. "Good riddance!" he snarled as he stomped back home to plan his next big crime.

'And that would have been the end of the story,' Loulou continued, 'if it hadn't been for the fact that many years later our own dear snuzzle, Katie, was out in the countryside on her bicycle when something caught her eye, something in an overgrown ditch that seemed to call to her. So she clambered off her bicycle and pushed her way through the long tangle of grass and what she found was a very old and very bedraggled rug. For a moment she almost threw it back but then something made her change her mind, something she couldn't really explain. You see, Katie Snuzzle, as we all know, is an artist and artists often see beauty and magic in things that other people would simply pass by.'

'But wait a minute!' Winnie exclaimed, cutting Loulou off in the middle of his story. 'I'm sorry to interrupt,' he said surprisingly politely, 'but the wizard and the robber lived in Zennadon and Katie lives in Limassol! How did the carpet get to Limassol?!'

'That's a very good question, young Winnie,' said Loulou, tapping the side of his nose. 'I was just coming to that. It's really very simple... You see, magic things and magic places and magic countries are all around us all the time but they are in what we call a different *Dimension*... So Zennadon is right here in dear old Limassol – invisible but as real as real can be!'

There was a short silence while Winnie absorbed this exciting piece of information. Just think! Every day he was walking in the magic places! What possibilities! A whole new world was opening up before him!

'Well, said Loulou, picking up the thread of his story, 'Katie carried the rug home on the back of her bicycle and the very next day she took it to a lady she had heard about who lived in the heart of old Limassol town and who was an expert carpet restorer, the very best in Cyprus.

'But not only was she the very best carpet restorer in Cyprus – in fact, in the whole world – but she was also a magical mystical sort of snuzzle and as soon as she saw the rug she instantly knew its whole history.

'She fetched her best gold thread and she mended the rug until it was as good as new, or even better – and she was the one who first sang that song you heard me sing earlier, the song of praise to the wizard's fabulous carpet.

'Well, Katie Snuzzle brought the carpet home, but she could never quite find the perfect place to show it off in all its glory (artists are very fussy like that) and so she rolled it up carefully and put it in a safe place in the hall. And then she forgot all about it and it has been here ever since.'

'So what does it do? What does it *do*?!' cried Winnie, whose patience had finally run out. He thought the story was very interesting but, after all, he was the one who had been bopped on the nose and the bum and he thought it was about time something actually *happened*. I mean, what's the point of a magic carpet if you don't *do* anything with it but just leave it sitting there in the hall all rolled up?

'What does it *do*?' he repeated. 'And what about my skink? He's still in there and I still want my game!'

Loulou sighed and shook his head:

'Winnie! You have a lot to learn! I promise you that if you will be patient for just a few more minutes I will not only *tell* you but will also *show* you what this marvellous carpet can do... But there are a couple more things you need to know first.'

Winnie pulled a face and rolled his eyes but settled back down obediently to listen.

Loulou still had his paw on the carpet and he looked long and hard at Winnie: 'First of all,' he said, 'there is a test you must do...'

Winnie wrinkled up his nose. 'A test?' he said. '*Me?*'

'Yes, *you!*' Loulou replied. 'Do you remember what I said about the carpet only being used for Good and that was why it didn't help the robber?'

Winnie nodded.

'Well,' Loulou went on, 'do you think that frightening Slinky Skinky who has never done you any harm is a kind thing to do? Would you call that *Good?*'

'I didn't want to *hurt* him, not really,' Winnie grumbled.

'I know,' Loulou replied, 'but you still can't expect the carpet to help you do something unkind.'

'Wasn't bopping my nose and my bum a bit unkind?' Winnie asked sulkily.

Loulou laughed. 'No! It didn't really hurt you and it was just trying to teach you an important lesson.'

'So what's this test then?' Winnie asked, keen to get it over with and find out what the carpet could do. It was all taking much longer than he thought was necessary. Honestly, grown-ups had no idea about what was really important...

'When I count to three,' Loulou said, 'Slinky Skinky is going to come out of his hiding place and he's going to slither *very slowly* past you, right under your nose. And you're going to sit very still and watch him and tell him you're sorry if you scared him...'

'Oh *no!*' Winnie whined. 'Do I *have* to?'

'No, you don't have to,' said Loulou calmly. 'But if you don't, you will never know anything more about the carpet and you will never have any of the fantastic adventures which it has got planned for you. The choice is yours...'

'Adventures!' Winnie squealed, his ears pricking up and his eyes big and bright.

'Yes! Adventures! – and lots of them,' Loulou said, nodding his head. 'So, are you ready?'

'Yes I'm ready,' Winnie said, suddenly feeling quite grown-up. He could apologise to Slinky Skinky if it meant having lots of adventures. In fact, he thought he could do just about *anything* if it meant having adventures and not having to snooze all day with nothing more than a mouldy old skink to chase when the others weren't looking.

Suddenly the rug gave a shake of its tassels and a little skink nose appeared at the entrance to its hiding place. Then a fat little body with stubby legs and finally a long long tail. Slinky Skinky looked directly at Winnie and then began to slither very slowly towards him until he was within nipping distance of Winnie's sharp teeth, and snatching distance of his sharp claws. Hissie and Sylvester held their breath. Hissie wasn't sure she really wanted to know what the carpet could do. But Sylvester, who was young at heart and a descendant of some extremely adventurous cats, was urging Winnie to do as he had been told.

And her prayers were answered because Winnie cleared his throat and said in a very calm voice: 'I apologise for giving you a fright Slinky Skinky. I will try not to do it again.'

(Of course, he had his paws crossed behind his back so it wasn't *really* a promise at all...)

'Thank you!' said the skink, and 'Well done!' said Loulou, and 'Good boy!' said Sylvester. And Hissie smiled a nervous little smile.

And then Skinky stuck his tongue out and ran right over Winnie's toes and out into the garden, chuckling a squeaky skinky chuckle as he ran to safety.

'Now!' squealed Winnie, jumping up and down. '*Now* tell me all about the carpet! You promised, Loulou, you *promised*...!'

'I did indeed!' said Loulou. 'But I also said I had to tell you a couple more very important little things...'

Winnie frowned but kept quiet.

'You remember I told you about the wizard who had made the carpet – and that the wizard had a very special cat – the noble Derrashah?'

Winnie nodded. 'Yes, Loulou, I remember,' he said politely.

'Well,' Loulou said, sitting up very straight and tall and proud, 'even Hissie and Sylvester don't know this but that famous wizard's cat was *me*! Correction: that famous wizard's cat *IS* me! – and I have known this carpet from its very first beginnings…'

'But *how*?!' Winnie exclaimed. 'I mean, I know you're very old and wise, Loulou, but I thought the wizard lived more than 100 years ago!'

'100 years is *nothing* for a wizard's cat!' Loulou said calmly. 'I have lived for thousands of years and I shall live for thousands of years more!'

'Amazing!' said Winnie; and 'My goodness me!' said Sylvester; and 'Oh dear oh dear!' said Hissie, 'I'm sure I feel quite faint.'

'You don't have to try to understand,' said Loulou kindly. 'Just know this: you will always be safe with me because I carry centuries of magical wisdom and power inside me. And that brings me to the most important thing of all…' He sat up even straighter than before and said, 'This carpet will follow *my* commands – and mine alone. I don't even have to speak – as soon as I think about what I want the carpet to do, it will obey me.'

Winnie looked forlorn. 'You mean it won't do what *I* want?' he asked in a miserable little voice.

'No!' said Loulou. 'At least, not yet… As you spend time with me, learning all I know, then maybe – just *maybe* – you will receive the magic key and be able to give your own orders to the carpet.'

'Cool!' said Winnie. 'And now, *please* make it *do* something!'

'Very well,' said Loulou. 'You've been extremely patient and have waited long enough.'

'Does it really fly?' asked Winnie, breathless with excitement.

'Of course it flies!' said Loulou. 'Whoever heard of a magic carpet that didn't fly?!'

'And can we have a fly *now*?!' Winnie asked. 'Right now, this very minute?!'

'I don't see why not,' said Loulou, who was beginning to enjoy himself. 'Do you think that's a good idea, ladies?'

'Definitely!' said Sylvester, but Hissie had gone quite pale and was beginning to feel all trembly and scared. Flying! Oh no! She didn't like the idea of flying! What if she felt sick or dizzy? What if she fell off? What if they never came home again?

'Don't worry, my dear,' said Loulou, putting a paw around Hissie's quaking shoulder. 'We won't fly very high the first time – just above the tops of the trees and the houses. And you'll be quite safe, I promise. And who knows, you might even like it!'

'Oh, I'm not sure,' Hissie said with a shudder, wringing her little paws. 'I don't know, truly I don't...'

She really didn't want to go but, on the other hand, it would be even worse to be left behind on her own.

So she sucked on one of her valerian pastilles (which are what moggies take to help them feel better when they are scared) and then she took a deep breath:

'All right!' she said. 'I'll come with you!'

'Bravo!' said Sylvester.

And then Loulou took command of the situation. 'Come along, everybody!' he said. 'Follow me! Chop chop!'

And he set off briskly out of the hall, with the others close behind.

'But what about the *carpet*?' Winnie cried. 'It's still in the hall, all rolled up!'

'That's what *you* think!' said Loulou with a grin, as they trotted out into the garden. 'What's *that* then...?!'

And the sight that met Winnie and Sylvester and Hissie's eyes made them all gasp in disbelief and delight.

Hovering three feet off the ground, right in the middle of the garden, was the most beautiful carpet any of them had ever seen. Its colours shone as bright as the sun and its tassels were golden, and its whole surface seemed to move and undulate like the swell of the sea on a summer's day. It looked friendly and inviting and occasionally gave a little dip and turn as if it were saying, 'Shall we dance?'

For a moment or two everyone stared without saying a word but then Winnie broke the silence:

'But how did it get here? And isn't it still rolled up in the hall anyway?'

Loulou laughed quietly. 'You remember I explained to you about the land of

Zennadon being right here in Limassol but in a different magic dimension? Well, it's the same with this beautiful carpet of ours. All magic carpets live *inside* ordinary carpets. The magic part slides in and out when it is needed. After all, if Katie Snuzzle went into the hall and the rug was missing she would know something was up. But now she will see that everything is as it always was, the carpet is still rolled up in the hall, nothing has changed. Magic adventures must be kept secret from snuzzles.'

'But some snuzzles are bound to see us when we go flying, aren't they?' said Winnie, with a worried expression on his long face. 'We can't always fly in places where there are no snuzzles, can we? And you told Hissie that we would fly low today so she needn't be worried...'

'Aah,' said Loulou in a low voice. 'That's one of the best things of all... Snuzzles can see the rug rolled up in the hall perfectly clearly but the magic part of the rug – this beautiful magic carpet you see in front of you now – is completely invisible to snuzzles! And as long as we're on the rug, *we* are invisible too! What do you think about *that*?!'

Winnie thought this was the most wonderful thing he had ever heard. They could go *anywhere*, they could do *anything* and nobody could see them! Surely he must be dreaming! What fun they would have! Surely even nervous Auntie Hissie wouldn't want to spend all her time snoozing when there was such fun to be had!

'Well,' said Loulou. 'There's no time like the present. It's time for what we aircraft captains call a Test Flight. Hissie and Sylvester, you can be in charge of safety and refreshments on board. And you, Winnie, will be my junior co-pilot – that means doing what you're told, understood?'

Winnie didn't think that sounded like much fun but Loulou quickly reassured him:

'Don't worry, young man,' he said, raising his eyebrows a little. 'I know you well enough to be sure you'll find plenty of opportunities for getting up to hijinks. Trust me, you won't be bored!'

And as soon as Sylvester had gathered together her first aid kit and Hissie had filled a picnic basket with delicious things to eat, and Loulou had presented Winnie with a smart cap which said Co-Pilot on the front, they all scrambled aboard.

Hissie was still feeling unsure and she gave a little squeak and a shriek as the carpet swayed a few inches to the left and then a few inches to the right. But, just as the magical carpet restorer had sung in her song, every stitch had a heart of gold and so the carpet understood her fear and it curled up its tassels all around the edge so nobody could fall off and Hissie immediately felt safe again.

'We'll soon be up, up and away!' cried Loulou. 'Let's all sing together now!' And they raised their voices to the heavens:

'Oh magic carpet so wise and old
 Tales of your courage will soon be told
 Of your hues so bright and rich and bold
 And of every stitch with its heart of gold...'

'Ooh!' thought Hissie happily, holding the picnic basket on her lap. 'I've read about lazy afternoons at the seaside! We can find a lovely quiet spot and I'll lay out the picnic things and Winnie can make sand castles.'

But, as you are about to discover, a lazy afternoon at the seaside was NOT what Hissie was going to have. Far from it! Unbeknownst to any of them (even Loulou), the Malekidi Moggies were just about to fly into their first Big Adventure... Hang on to your hat! It's time for take-off...

3

A TURTLE IN THE SOUP

A very strange sound was coming from Katie Snuzzles's garden. It was the sound of four moggies and zillions of *ziziros* and beetles and other buzzing insects all counting backwards in very loud voices. Even Slinky Skinky had joined in, along with a couple of passing seagulls.

This was because Loulou had announced that there must be a proper countdown for the first flight of the Magical Malekidi Carpet – just like when snuzzles sent a rocket up into space.

'Ten – nine – eight…!' they all shouted.

'Seven – six – five…!' they shouted louder still.

Even Hissie's voice was as loud as Winnie's because she was shaking with fright and it was the only way she could stop herself from fainting.

'Four – three – two!' they cried as Winnie did a double somersault and Loulou squared his shoulders and Sylvester held on to her straw hat. Hissie dug her claws into the picnic basket and shut her eyes tight.

'One!' chorused all the voices and then Loulou made the final command in his most captain-like voice, 'Lift off!'

And with a great *Whoosh!* up went the carpet – up and up and up, until it was 20 feet above the top of the tallest tree in the garden.

'Oh, look!' squealed Sylvester excitedly. 'Come on, Hissie! Open your eyes – I'll hold your paw.'

They were hovering above the highest tree

COPILOT

And even though she was scared half to death, Hissie didn't want to be the only one not joining in and so she held tight to Sylvester's paw and peeked over the edge.

'Oh!' she gasped. 'How beautiful!'

And it was.

From up here Katie Snuzzles's garden looked like a garden in a fairytale – all the leaves shimmering in the afternoon sunshine and the colourful mosaics sparkling and seeming to dance. All the flies and *ziziros* and beetles looked up and waved and cheered and Slinky Skinky ran up to the top of the lemon tree and poked his long tongue out at Winnie.

But Winnie didn't care. He was *flying*! Nothing, especially not a silly old skink, was going to spoil the best day of his life.

Soon they were hovering above the highest tree, all of them peeking over the edge with their hearts in their mouths as they caught their first glimpse of the sparkling blue sea.

'That was what is known as a Perfectly Smooth Take-off,' said Captain Loulou proudly. 'Now – away we go on our maiden flight...!'

Try as he might, Winnie found he simply couldn't behave like a sensible, serious co-pilot. He was very proud of his smart cap with its gold braid and it made him look very grown-up and handsome and important but all he really wanted to do was have fun.

The carpet rose higher and higher into the blue sky and Loulou sighed and shook his head as Winnie did six press-ups just to show off how muscly he was and bounced up and down as if the carpet were a trampoline and finally leapt right off the edge and hung on by one claw so that he was stretched out behind, flying through the air like Superman.

'Don't worry, Loulou,' said Sylvester in her soothing old-lady's voice. 'We all know that Winnie's too young to behave properly so why don't we just let him do as he wants so that he learns a few lessons the hard way?' Then she smiled and said with a twinkle in her eye, '*You* were young once too, Loulou, and I remember hearing some hair-raising stories of things *you* got up to in your youth...!'

And if Loulou had not been an all-black cat, he would have blushed as Sylvester said this because, yes, he had to admit he had been just as much of a daredevil as Winnie and it was easy to forget that Winnie, too, would one day grow up into a wise old cat. *Or would he..?!* Loulou wondered. It's true that he himself had done some crazy things in his early years but he had never completely disappeared off a magic carpet...

For, yes, that is exactly what Winnie had done! One minute he had been flying along being Superman and the next he had completely vanished...

By this time the carpet was sailing happily along high above the treetops of the beautiful mile-long promenade (which in Limassol is called The Molos and runs all the way along the seashore) and Hissie had actually begun to enjoy herself. There was a gentle sea breeze and she was enthralled by the scene below. There were people strolling along in colourful t-shirts and sun hats; there were swimmers bobbing about in the sea, squealing with delight; there were cars and bicycles and big blue buses whizzing along; there were beautiful gardens filled with flowers and trees and pieces of interesting sculpture; and there were snuzzles sitting on benches eating ice cream.

Hissie was looking forward to setting out the tea things from the picnic hamper and she was humming and smiling to herself. And the thing that made her hum and smile the most was that she, Hissie, scaredy-cat Hissie, was actually sitting on a magic carpet high up in the air! She could hardly believe it! She had never been so far away from home before and she felt proud and calm.

At least, she *had* felt proud and calm until it became clear that Winnie was nowhere on board. Loulou and Sylvester had hunted high and low to see if he could be playing hide-and-seek with them but, no, he had disappeared into thin air.

'Oh where can he be?' Hissie fretted. 'He could be *anywhere!*'

And as she looked down at the cars and buses and busy pavements below, she started to shake again.

Winnie was naughty and he drove them all mad with his pranks but what if he were lost for ever? She couldn't bear the thought of life without Winnie and she quite forgot all about the lovely picnic she had planned.

Once again, Loulou put his big furry arm around her quaking shoulders and said:

'There, there, Hissie, you can relax and stop worrying, you really can.'

'B-but how can you be sure,' Hissie asked in a very small voice. 'He's so naughty and he could get himself into danger…'

'That's true,' Loulou admitted. 'But he's not in any danger now, I promise you.'

'But *how* can you promise such a thing?' Hissie wailed.

'Because the carpet would have told me!' he replied as if it were the most natural thing in the world. 'Our magic carpet is perfectly designed to look after us – *all* of us, even Winnie! – especially Winnie! *Now* can you relax?!'

Hissie dried her eyes and smiled. 'Oh yes, Loulou! I see. Yes, I do quite understand now. Oh, what a relief! Shall I make us all a cup of tea and we can go and look for him in a little while?'

'That's an excellent idea,' said Loulou, and five minutes later the three grown-ups were enjoying catnip tea and salmon sandwiches with cream cheese, as if they hadn't a care in the world.

Loulou instructed the carpet to take them on a gentle ride over the beach and a short way out over the little waves. And because they were invisible they could stay low enough to enjoy all the goings-on without any of the snuzzles knowing they were there.

It was great fun. They felt completely safe and the catnip tea had made them just a little bit snoozy which is one of the most delicious feelings in the world (especially when you're a grown-up).

Through their drowsy eyes they laughed at the sight of the snuzzles splashing each other and screaming when they saw a jellyfish, and falling off their lilos, and doing all the sorts of other things which snuzzles do when they're on their holidays.

Sylvester insisted that Loulou tell the carpet to dip right down so that they could all trail their paws in the cool blue water and even Hissie enjoyed it, especially when Sylvester started to tell them about her great great great great great great great Uncle Vanya:

'We called him Uncle Van for short,' she said, 'and that was quite right because he was one of the famous Van cats from Turkey which actually *swim*! Oh yes, they're very famous, the Van cats, they absolutely *love* getting in the water and no snuzzle has ever been able to explain how this came to be. Anyway, my Uncle Van was *such* a handsome gentleman!' Sylvester went on. 'He had long white fur and black ears and a black face and a black tail – *very* distinguished! And, most marvellous of all, his eyes were different colours! – one was blue and the other was amber! *My* coat, as you can all see, is almost entirely black (that's from my mother's side of the family) but I've inherited my Uncle Van's love of water.'

'Yes,' said Loulou, nodding his head. 'I've seen you sometimes jump right into the water butt in the garden when you thought nobody was looking!'

'Oh no!' Sylvester cried. 'I thought you would laugh at me so I've tried to keep it a secret all these years...'

'We wouldn't have laughed,' Loulou assured her, and Hissie nodded in agreement. 'Of course we wouldn't.'

'In fact,' Sylvester said with a gleam in her eye, 'I'm very tempted to jump into the sea this very minute to practise my backstroke...'

'No, not just here,' Loulou said firmly. 'There are too many snuzzles about and I feel responsible for you. I'm sorry my dear but my mind's made up – you'll have to wait for another opportunity.'

Reluctantly Sylvester agreed. She was longing to dive in but, like Hissie, she knew that when Loulou told you what to do in that firm voice, you really should do as you were told. Loulou always knew best.

So now, let's leave Hissie, Sylvester and Loulou to enjoy the rest of their tea and their gentle flight over the beach and go and see if we can track down Winnie.

Ah yes! Sure enough, he'd been busy having an adventure.

This is what had happened:

As he was sailing along doing his Superman impression, the most mouthwatering aroma of chicken kebab had reached his long nose and he simply had to see where it was coming from. And there, just below him was a fat lady snuzzle sitting under a tree tucking into the juiciest kebab he had ever seen or smelt. And before he knew what he was doing, he had let go of the carpet, landed on the grass, swiped a piece of chicken and made a run for it.

What he had forgotten was that the minute he left the carpet he was no longer invisible and an almighty hue and cry ensued. The fat lady started screaming in Greek and then her husband jumped up and started chasing Winnie and all of a sudden the young scamp had twenty excited Cypriot snuzzles chasing after him all along The Molos and, what's more, they were running much faster than he would have expected...

Just as he was beginning to feel tired and even beginning to regret diving for the piece of chicken which he was still clutching in his paw, he heard a loud 'Psssst! Up here! Quick!'

Looking up, Winnie could just make out some sort of a cat in a blue and white stripey t-shirt at the top of a very tall Norfolk Island pine tree. He didn't hesitate. In five seconds flat he was up the trunk and all the way to the top and out along one of the scratchy branches. And finally, cheeky so-and-so that he was, he took a bite of the chicken and then nonchalantly dropped the rest of it so it landed right on the fat Cypriot lady snuzzle's head. This made her scream even louder but Winnie didn't care. He was safe now and,

besides, he had returned the stolen property (or at least most of it) to its rightful owner so what did she have to complain about? And

he waggled his bum and stuck his tongue out, which is an extremely rude and naughty thing to do.

He then put all thoughts of snuzzles and kebabs out of his mind and turned his attention to his rescuer who was shinning along the branch towards him.

'Well, thanks very much,' the stranger said grumpily. 'I'm *starving*! You might have kept some of that kebab for me instead of chucking it all away like that...'

Winnie felt very small all of a sudden, all of his bravado had vanished in a puff of smoke. This chap in front of him wasn't as big as Loulou but he did look pretty rough, the sort you don't mess about with.

'I'm very s-s-sorry,' he said in a very humble voice, most unlike his usual stroppy self, 'r-r-r-eally sorry...'

'No harm done,' the other replied in a much friendlier manner. 'The truth is I'd have done exactly the same meself at your age. My name's Plug, by the way, what's yours?'

'Winnie,' said Winnie. And then added, '*Co-pilot* Winnie...'

'Yeah, I saw your carpet,' Plug said in a rough but approving tone of voice. 'Not bad, not bad at all. Where are you headed?'

'Nowhere in particular,' Winnie answered truthfully. 'This is our first flight – a test flight.'

'Aah!' said Plug, giving his whiskers a twirl and spitting out a bit of catnip tobacco he had been chewing. 'Do you reckon you could give me a lift?'

'Oh yes!' said Winnie, 'I'm sure Captain Loulou and the ladies would be very happy to have you on board.'

Actually, he wasn't at all sure about this because, even to Winnie's eyes, Plug looked like a very rough diamond.

He was extremely grizzled and his blue and white stripey t-shirt was tattered and none too clean over his dusty ginger coat. Then there was the fact that both his ears were chewed up and battle-scarred, he only had one eye and he had a habit of wiping his nose on the back of his paw. Even Winnie could see he wasn't exactly polished and he knew how fussy the ladies, especially Hissie, were about tomcats being neat and tidy. And as for Loulou, well, he was always telling Winnie off for his bad manners, and Winnie was pretty sure that Plug's manners would leave a lot to be desired.

But the truth was that Winnie already thought Plug was the bee's knees. You could just tell by looking at him that he'd had hundreds and thousands of Big Adventures and could tell you loads of wonderful stories. In fact, he was just the sort of grown-up cat that Winnie would like to grow up into. And, on top of everything, Plug had saved him from all those furious snuzzles so Loulou and the ladies would jolly well have to give him a lift if he wanted one.

It so happened that at that very moment the carpet appeared above them as if by magic and Captain Loulou called out:

'Ahoy there! You seem to have given refuge to our missing co-pilot!' he said to Plug in a friendly tone of voice. 'I imagine you got him out of some sort of mischief...'

But before Plug could answer, Winnie chimed in:

'This is my new friend Mr Plug and he saved me from some terrible snuzzles who were chasing me for no reason at all and I told him you would be happy to show your gratitude by giving him a lift on our carpet...' The words came out all in a rush.

'And this time it was Plug's turn to speak before Loulou had had a chance to say a word:

'The thing is, Sir, I was on an errand ashore and my boat sailed without me. That's my boat way out there,' he said, waving a scraggy paw towards the horizon. 'It's a fishing vessel and I've been the ship's cat for eight years now and I've never missed the boat before. They'll be frantic without me...'

Loulou turned to Sylvester and Hissie who had been whispering together. He could see that Hissie was worried by Plug's shabby appearance but he could also see that Sylvester was very keen to say something.

'What is it, Sylvester?' he asked.

'May I ask Mr Plug a question?' she said.

'Yes, of course,' Loulou replied.

'Very well,' Sylvester said. 'Have you ever heard of Vanya the Valiant?'

Plug's eyes instantly lit up like fireworks. 'Vanya the Valiant? – the swimming cat?!' he exclaimed. 'Well of course I have! There isn't a seafaring cat in the Mediterranean who hasn't heard of Vanya the Valiant! Why do you ask?'

'He was my great great great great great great great uncle!' Sylvester said with pride.

'Oh, Madam, let me shake you by the paw!' Plug said with a beaming smile. 'This is a rare honour...'

And Winnie watched in amazement as the old sea-cat switched on the charm and in no time at all had won over both ladies. *This is an important thing to remember,* Winnie said to himself. *It doesn't matter what you look like as long as you know how to say the right thing at the right time...*

'Well, well, well!' laughed Loulou. 'Any cat who holds a relation of Sylvester's in such high regard certainly deserves a lift! Welcome aboard, Mr Plug – we'll get you to your boat in a jiffy.'

'That's exceedingly kind of you,' said Plug with warmth as he jumped from the tree on to the hovering carpet. 'And don't worry, ladies, you won't go home empty-handed. As soon as we get to the boat I'll make sure you've got plenty of fresh sardines to take home with you – the freshest you've ever tasted – and maybe some mullet as well!'

Winnie was delighted. Not only had all the grown-ups welcomed his fascinating new friend aboard but they seemed to have forgotten all about his naughtiness in leaping off the carpet in the first place. Phew! Now he could get back to the important business of enjoying the rest of the afternoon.

The carpet sailed higher and higher into the blue sky so they could look down and see all the snuzzles getting smaller and smaller until they were just lots of coloured dots bobbing about far below them. Then, as they headed out to sea in the direction of Plug's boat, they began to notice the different colours in the water – every shade of blue and green from turquoise to emerald, from lime to deep purple. And the surface of the sea was flecked with millions and zillions of tiny white waves which Plug explained were known as white horses because they looked like pure white ponies tossing their manes and galloping forwards on the water.

He knew the sea so well and he described the boats and rocks and shoals of fish in such an interesting and exciting way that even Hissie forgot to be afraid as they all peered over the edge and looked down at the scene beneath. And nobody objected to the fact that every now and again the grizzled old sea-cat spat a little piece of chewed-up catnip tobacco over the side. They had all accepted that that's what seafaring folk do.

Plug pointed out all the currents in the water, the way they swirled and curled and changed colour and direction like huge sea-snakes travelling this way and that. 'They can be very strong,' he said, 'you don't want to get caught in one of those...'

And even Sylvester, with her great love of water, shuddered for a moment at the thought of being swept along by such a strong, fierce flow.

But just as they began to relax and enjoy the scene again, Plug suddenly stretched right out over the edge and shouted, '*That* shouldn't be there! There's something wrong down there! Come and look! See what I mean?'

And as the others strained their eyes in the direction he was pointing, they could clearly see a small speck right in the middle of a swirling current.

'What is it?' they all said in unison. 'Do you know what it is, Plug?'

'I can't tell from up here,' he said in a very concerned voice. 'Captain Loulou, would you be so good as to instruct the carpet to dip down closer to the surface of the water so we can see more clearly? I'm sure somebody's in danger!'

Loulou immediately did as Plug had asked and in no time at all the carpet was gently descending over the current and getting closer to where the little speck was flailing around.

'Yes!' Plug cried. 'It's a turtle! Look! She's been carried off-course by the current. She must be trying to get to her breeding ground. That's what they do at this time of year. All the lady turtles return to the beach where they themselves were hatched. And that's where they lay their eggs and later their babies break out of their shells and hurry down to the sea to begin their lives. My guess is that she was heading for Shipwreck Bay with a lot of her friends and relations but that somehow she got separated from them and this huge current is sweeping her away. She must be exhausted! If we don't rescue her quickly she will certainly drown... Oh, Captain Loulou, drowning is a horrible way to die! I implore you to instruct the carpet to dive right down to the water so we can save her life – and the lives of her babies too! I can tell that this is a magnificent carpet and that you are a magnificent captain and that the ladies would want to save another lady and that Winnie will behave himself in this crisis... *Please* give the order!'

Loulou didn't hesitate. He knew it would be a risk – especially when this was meant to be just a test flight – but there are times in Life when 'a cat's gotta do what a cat's gotta do' and he was wise enough to know that this was one of those times.

At Loulou's silent command, the carpet immediately began to make a swift and smooth descent. The white horses got bigger and bigger and the sparkles on the water got brighter and brighter as the carpet got closer to the surface of the sea.

They were all peering over the edge now and they could see quite clearly that Plug was absolutely right. A big green turtle was spluttering and trying desperately to swim against the pull of the current but her task was hopeless. They could see that she was completely exhausted, she had no strength left in her body and was being pulled and dragged along to certain death.

Once again and without a moment's hesitation, Winnie leapt over the side and hung on to the edge by one claw as he tried to reach out to the floundering turtle with his other arm.

'Oh Winnie, *do* be careful!' gasped Hissie, whose fearfulness had returned even more strongly. '*Do* take care!' And she put her paws over her eyes and started to say her prayers.

The next thing was that Sylvester had dived in and was swimming frantically round and round in circles trying to grab hold of the turtle. But moggies are very small and green turtles are very big and so, even with Plug calling out encouragement to them, they had no chance at all of rescuing the poor creature.

And then things got even worse because Winnie's claw couldn't hold on any longer and he fell into the water with an enormous splash. And, unlike Sylvester, Winnie didn't have any swimming ancestors in his family so he didn't have a clue how to stay afloat and he found himself sinking down, down, down into the water which was surprisingly cold and dark.

Thank goodness that Captain Loulou had learnt over many years how to keep cool in a crisis. He calmly conveyed his instructions to the carpet and the magnificent rug dipped its edge right down into the water and in one smooth, swift movement scooped up all three of the bedraggled animals: Winnie, Sylvester and one very big, very frightened and very grateful turtle.

Winnie and Sylvester shook their fur and gave each other a quick lick so they didn't look so dishevelled, and Plug and Loulou congratulated them for their courage (although, to be honest, they both thought that Sylvester and Winnie had been pretty stupid to imagine they could haul the huge turtle out of the water on their own).

But this was no time to criticise. All their attention now was on the big unfamiliar lady who was lying, too exhausted to move, in the middle of the carpet which had risen a few yards up into the air again and was rocking gently back and forth in just the right way to soothe everybody on board.

Hissie had swung into action and was pouring strong sweet tea into the picnic cups. Plug took a cup in his big tatty paws and gently spooned a few drops into the turtle's mouth which looked dry and cracked.

'Come on, Madam,' he said with a sense of urgency in his voice. 'Try to swallow a little. You *must* do as I say so that you can begin to get your strength back...'

Winnie and Sylvester and Hissie looked on anxiously and even Loulou had a very concerned expression on his face. They were afraid the exertion had been too much for her.

'She's very young,' whispered Plug. 'This is definitely her first year of laying eggs – we must think very positively and imagine sending her lots and lots of strength and energy...'

They all closed their eyes tight shut and did as Plug had commanded (even Loulou didn't mind taking orders for once) and 20 seconds later they heard a rattling sigh and saw the turtle's eyes flicker and open a little.

'She's coming round!' shouted Plug in delight.

'Hurray!' shouted Winnie, dancing from one foot to the other.

'Oh, that's wonderful!' exclaimed Sylvester.

'Excellent, excellent!' boomed Loulou.

And Hissie just wiped away a tear because she was so relieved she couldn't speak.

An hour later the scene was very different. They had learnt that the lady's name was Myrtle Turtle and that, just as Plug had suggested earlier, she had been on her way to Shipwreck Bay and this was her first season for laying eggs.

Hissie had dried Myrtle's shell and rubbed in some of the special oil she always carried with her and Sylvester had massaged her flippers... Plug had sung her an encouraging sea shanty... Loulou had assured her that the carpet would get her to Shipwreck Bay in double quick time... And Winnie had made her laugh by chasing his tail and pulling faces at the same time. And, as we all know, laughter is the best medicine so by the time the carpet sailed off in the direction of the beach, Myrtle was feeling stronger and happier than she had felt in a very long time.

By now they could clearly see the shipwreck beneath them – the shipwreck after which the bay was named. And Plug turned to them and spoke in a sombre voice:

'I always feel sad when I see a shipwreck,' he said. 'This one here was called The Gurden Gates and 70 years ago she was a proud and magnificent cargo ship taking urgent supplies across the Atlantic Ocean. This was during the terrible Snuzzle War that was going on at that time and she served her country, which was Great Britain, faithfully for six years. But then she was sold several times to different owners and they kept changing her name, which is Very Bad Luck for a ship and that's why in 1967 she ran aground right here and this is all that's left of her. By then, she was called The Three Stars.'

They all stared for a moment at the rusting hulk sticking out of the water and they felt sad too, especially when Plug continued: 'And, remember, that every single ship has a ship's cat or cats so they probably drowned and I always spend a moment's silence in memory of the lost ship's cats every time I see a shipwreck.'

They all bowed their heads for a moment but by then the carpet was almost at the shoreline and they knew it was time to say Farewell to Myrtle.

'I don't know *how* I can repay you!' she said as she looked out and saw her friends and relations all gathered there, waiting for her.

'There's no need to repay us, my dear,' Loulou said kindly. 'The Malekidi Moggies – and Mr Plug here – are always happy to help a stranger in distress…'

But the young turtle looked at him through her steady green eyes and said firmly:

'I *shall* repay you one day. I don't know how or when or where but I *shall*…'

And Loulou brushed a gentlemanly kiss on her outstretched flipper.

'Oh!' she exclaimed in a voice full of happiness. 'There's my mother!' And she waved at an even bigger turtle who had been digging a hole for her eggs. 'Hello Mum!' she shouted, 'I'm safe! These wonderful moggies saved my life and here I am!'

They all knew there wasn't a moment to lose. Myrtle needed to get on to the sand as quickly as possible to prepare to lay her eggs as soon as the sun went down.

She waved at an even bigger tu

who had been digging a hole for her eggs

The carpet settled on the beach and she slid away towards her friends and her mother (who were all crying tears of joy and relief).

'She'll be safe now,' Plug said with a satisfied smile. 'That was a job well done!'

'Hear hear!' said Loulou.

'Hear hear!' everyone else agreed.

'And now, off to Mr Plug's boat!' commanded Loulou. 'What a busy and adventurous test flight this has been!'

And immediately the carpet lifted itself up into the air once more and set its course in the direction of the fishing boat on the horizon.

By now everyone had got used to Plug and as his boat came closer into view each and every one of them felt a little sad that they would be saying Goodbye to him so soon.

The ladies had enjoyed his gentlemanly manners which were such a surprise when you looked at his tattered ears and his scraggy whiskers, and Winnie loved his stories and the way he knew so much about this and that and what time the tides came in and went out. He even knew which seaweed tasted good with fresh sardines and had given Hissie a recipe to try. And Loulou had enjoyed having another man about the place for a change (Winnie was still very much a boy so he didn't count). He would have loved to sit down with Plug and have a man-to-man chat over something stronger than catnip tea. Loulou loved Hissie and Sylvester very much but sometimes he did feel rather outnumbered by having two ladies and no other grown-up chaps to spend time with.

'Isn't she a beauty?' Plug said proudly when the carpet was finally hovering right above his boat which was brightly painted in blue and yellow and white and red. 'She's called *Oi Tharalea Thalessea Gáta* which is Greek for *The Courageous Sea-Cat.*' He paused, deep in thought, for a moment and then added, 'They named her after me, you know, when I was three years old. I had been their ship's cat in their previous boat and I'd kept my head during a dreadfully fierce storm which almost wrecked the boat and endangered all our lives. So when they built this new beautiful boat they named her after me. I'm 12 now, quite a good age, eh?'

He gazed down at the fishing smack. 'She's my home!' he said fondly, 'not just my place of work. I know every inch of her and woe betide any mice or rats who think it would be a good idea to sneak aboard for a feast of fish or leftovers from the fishermen's lunch! I caught my 350th rat last week! Just think of that! I keep a scorecard beside my bunk.'

'Ooh!' cried Winnie, 'do you sleep in a bunk?!'

'Of course I do. All seafaring folk – snuzzles as well as moggies – sleep in a bunk or a hammock. It's a grand life, young Winnie, the salty air in your lungs, a diet of the best fish in the world, and the company of three great guys: Yiannos, Panos and Phanos!'

Winnie was in raptures.

'I'd *love* to be a ship's cat when I'm properly grown up!' he said. 'That's what I'm going to be!'

'Honestly, Winnie!' Loulou said with a frown and a smile both at the same time. 'You've just become my co-pilot on the most magnificent magic carpet in the whole Mediterranean and already you're thinking of something more exciting…!'

'I'm sorry, Captain Loulou,' Winnie said politely. 'I didn't mean to be rude. Perhaps I could be a ship's cat at weekends?'

And they all laughed.

Plug couldn't hang around any longer to chat. 'There's work to be done,' he explained apologetically, 'and I've lost a couple of hours already. I don't like to let Yiannos and Panos and Phanos down – they all work so hard and they count on me to do my bit. They're very good to me.'

Everyone said that of course they understood but that they would all miss him and they made him promise to come and visit them one day when the boat was in Limassol harbour.

'That would be wonderful!' said Plug. 'I'll definitely do that and I'm sure Miss Hissie will make some of her delicious tea and Miss Sylvester will show me the water butt where she practises her swimming!'

Hissie and Sylvester beamed and blushed and promised they would.

'Now, just give me half a minute,' Plug said as he leapt off the carpet and scampered along the deck. He quickly returned bearing armfuls of sardines and prawns and calamari and some of the special seaweed from his own store, along with half a bottle of Heinz tomato ketchup as an extra treat. And then, almost before they had had time to thank him, he had disappeared into the boat and set to work.

An hour later the adventurous moggies were all stretched out on the roof of the lovely house in Malekidi Street. 'Home sweet home!' sighed Hissie. 'What a day!'

And Katie Snuzzle was very puzzled when she came home to discover that none of them wanted any dinner.

'I hope they're not ill,' she said to herself. 'I expect it's just that they haven't done anything to work up an appetite. I'm pretty sure they've all been sleeping on the roof all day – what a lazy lot!'

But she *was* rather perplexed by the strong smell of fish in the garden and then she found a pawprint on the path which was definitely made out of tomato ketchup…

But when she came back with a cloth to wipe it up a couple of minutes later, she found that it had completely disappeared.

'How odd,' she thought. 'Oh well, I must have imagined it…'

(Of course she didn't see Winnie peeping out from behind the compost heap with a gleam in his eye and a smear of tomato ketchup on his lips.)

And as soon as the sun had gone down the Malekidi Moggies all found themselves yawning much more than usual – even Winnie.

Loulou filled in his Captain's log book, describing all the doings of the day and Sylvester snuggled down, remembering how lovely the sea water had felt on her fur, even though it *had* been a bit scary. And Hissie's heart was still beating a little faster than usual because she had had a Real Proper Adventure and she had enjoyed the company of a gentleman sailor cat who had made her feel special. And she said a prayer for dear Myrtle Turtle and hoped that all her eggs would hatch safely and that they would all meet again one day.

And Winnie stretched out under the stars and, even though he was very sleepy, he was also bright-eyed with the excitement of it all. And let's be honest, it was all because of *him*! If he hadn't chased Slinky Skinky none of this would have happened. That made him very happy and he started to doze off, imagining himself in his Superman cape performing great feats of derring-do.

'And, best of all,' he said to himself just before sleep overcame him, 'This is just the *Beginning...*!'

4

THE CAT'S WHISKERS

Winnie had certainly been right when he'd told himself that the Big Adventure with Myrtle Turtle was only the beginning but, if he had realised how much growing up he would have to do over the next six months and how many new moggies he would meet (some very nice and some truly horrible), it would have made his head spin. He wouldn't have believed it.

Perhaps it's just as well that none of us knows what is right around the corner...

For the first couple of days after the Big Turtle Rescue, Winnie's bouncy energy was all used up. His tank was completely empty and he was content to snooze the days away, going over every exciting detail in his mind. Again and again he relived the exhilaration of whizzing over the sea on the magic carpet and he remembered how happy he had felt to see Myrtle safely back on her special beach. And he chuckled to himself as he replayed in his mind the way he had so cheekily snatched that lady snuzzle's kebab... He liked that memory best of all. 'I must do it again one day,' he said to himself with a wicked gleam in his eye.

But after two days of being lazy and lying about in the sun daydreaming he was once again bursting with bounce, eager for another dollop of fun. It was definitely time for Something New but, as usual, Loulou, Hissie and Sylvester had turned back into boring old grown-ups who weren't interested in any of his great ideas.

'Let's go to England on the carpet!' he suggested, as he swung from the gutter by one back foot. 'Or China! Or the North Pole! What about checking that the turtle eggs are safe? We could have a gymnastics competition for me and all the other young dudes in Malekidi Street! Or we could go and collect loads of pretty shells for Katie Snuzzle's garden. She'd like that...' And he spun around and did two cartwheels.

But, no. All his ideas fell on deaf ears so that he began to feel himself getting grumpy and bored all over again.

But not for long...

The very next morning he pulled himself together. He ya..ned and stretched and he pounded his fists on his chest.

'All right,' he said under his breath, so that Loulou and the others couldn't hear. 'If you lot don't want to do anything more interesting than snoozing and washing and lying about on the roof 24 hours a day, I'll just have to make my own fun, *won't I?!*'

And that was how he came to discover The Cat's Whiskers...

The Cat's Whiskers was a nightclub, set up in an old deserted house with a tangled garden in the next street to Malekidi Street. Even before the adventure with Myrtle Turtle, Winnie had often lain awake at night listening to the strange and thrilling sounds coming from that direction and wondering what they were. There was loud singing and lots of weird banging and crashing and caterwauling which went on from midnight till six in the morning. After that, it all went quiet – so quiet in fact that Winnie often wondered if he had dreamt it. And when he mentioned it a couple of times to the others, they all said he didn't know what he was talking about and it was all in his imagination.

But now, as he thought about it again, he realised he didn't believe them. He felt sure they were keeping quiet about something. 'I bet they know and just aren't telling me,' he told himself. 'Hmmmm... We'll just have to see about that, won't we?'

So the next night, when the grown-ups had been particularly boring and Winnie was particularly wide awake with his new sense of determination, he felt a delicious itchiness in his paw-pads. Yes! It was time to go and investigate...

To be on the safe side, he put on his co-pilot's cap, the one Loulou had given him on their test flight. He was very excited at the thought of sneaking out at night on his own but he was also a tiny bit frightened and putting on the cap somehow made him feel stronger and braver.

He had learned to move silently, so none of the others heard him in the darkness as he slid off the roof and down the tree and into the garden and then squeezed under the back gate. He sniffed the air and trotted off in the direction of the singing and banging and crashing. And even though he could hear all sorts of interesting squeaking and scratching noises coming from the tussocks of scrubby grass as he crossed the small area of open ground behind Katie Snuzzle's house, he didn't let himself get sidetracked. No! He was a young man on a mission and, with his heart hammering in his chest, he continued in the direction of the intriguing sounds which were now getting even louder – deafening, in fact – as he approached the next street.

A couple of minutes later Winnie was crouching in front of an old rusty gate with spikes on the top. Peering through in the darkness with his extra-special night vision (which all cats have), he could make out about a dozen dustbins behind a tangle of overgrown shrubs. He could also see the moving shapes of 50 or more cats jiggling about, waving their front paws in the air, bushing up their tails and yowling. Two or three of them were pounding their paws on the dustbins, making a tremendous racket which made Winnie want to join in with the dancing and jiggling about. This looked like fun! This was more like it! And he was just about to squeeze through the railings when a gruff voice in his ear made him jump out of his skin:

'And what have we got here?!' the voice boomed, and Winnie found himself being unceremoniously picked up by the scruff of his neck and dangled over the top of the gate, with those nasty spikes digging into his soft tummy. 'We seem to have an uninvited guest!' the voice went on and Winnie was suddenly staring into the gleaming orange eyes of the biggest, scruffiest, most battle-scarred ginger cat he had ever seen. This fellow made Plug look positively polished and suave.

'Er, er...' Winnie stuttered, 'I was only having a look... I heard the noises and I couldn't sleep so I thought I'd come and have a look...'

'Oh, you did, *did you*,' came the surly reply. 'Come to cause trouble, more like...'

'No, no,' said Winnie in a shaky voice, 'I didn't mean any trouble, honest, I'll go home if you want me to...'

By this time, half a dozen other scruffy mogs had wandered over to see what the fuss was about. 'Give him a kick in the bum!' shouted out one voice... 'Bite off his ear!' came another. 'Cheeky young scallywag, let *me* have a go at him...' hissed another, who was very drunk and looked decidedly dangerous.

This wasn't what Winnie had imagined at all and he felt himself sweating and beginning to panic. The spikes on the gate were very sharp – and so were the teeth and claws of the ugly bunch surrounding him. But then all of a sudden another voice cut through the din:

'Put him down, you big bully! He's only a kid... Let's have a look at him...'

So that is how Winnie came to be jigging up and down.....

And the next thing was that Winnie was being dropped from a great height and he landed with a thud on the hard ground. Ouch! And, as he scrambled to his feet, he found himself looking up at a very fat elderly lady-cat, who was holding a champagne glass in one paw and a cigarette holder in the other. There were tiny diamante beads on the tips of her ears, and her whiskers were purple. She had a shawl made out of chicken feathers around her shoulders and, most important of all, she had a kind face and she smiled.

'So what's your name then, lad?' she asked, 'Mine's Big Mamma and I'm pleased to meet you.'

'W.. W.. Winnie,' said Winnie. 'I didn't mean any trouble, Big Mamma, I was bored and I just wanted to come and find some fun...'

'Well, you've come to the right place!' said Big Mamma with a laugh. 'And don't you take any notice of this riffraff...' she added, jerking her big head in the direction of the boozy bullies at the gate. 'I like your style – especially that cute cap of yours – and this is my joint so what I say goes, right?'

'Right!' said Winnie with a grin of relief.

'Right!' muttered the others.

'You are now a life member of The Cat's Whiskers Club so come on in and have a drink.'

And that is how Winnie came to be jigging up and down with a glass of catnip whisky in one hand and a mouseburger in the other while the band (which was called the Malekidi Monsters) crashed out their rhythm on the dustbin lids and a skinny black lady cat in a green lizard-skin minidress wailed out a song about a no-good guy called Ted.

Winnie thought he had died and gone to Heaven. This was the life! Lots of new 'edgy' friends who kept saying he was cute and they liked his style, and plenty of opportunities to show off, plus an endless supply of junk food. And of course there were lots and lots of pretty girl-cats. What more could a young dude ask for?

And so it was that, night after night for almost three weeks, Winnie sneaked under the back gate and down to The Cat's Whiskers to drink and dance the night away.

And the cherry on the cake was that Fat Tom the barman (who had once been a prize sumo wrestler) took a shine to him and always served him double measures of drinks even though he only ever charged him for singles. This was *living*!

Winnie quickly discovered that he was very popular with the ladies and this encouraged him to take his showing-off to new heights. He watched in fascination as a couple of Jamaican cats demonstrated limbo dancing and in no time at all he had joined in and quite a crowd had gathered. He found that he was able to bend himself almost double and on only his third night of trying, he won the limbo dancing competition by managing to wriggle underneath a limbo pole which was only six inches off the ground.

'Ooh!' and 'Aah!' squealed the little crowd of girl-cats who had gathered round. 'Isn't he clever?!' they whispered to each other as Winnie wiggled and wriggled and squirmed on the dancefloor. 'And isn't he handsome?!' and 'I wish he would dance with *me...*'

On another occasion and after several glasses of catnip whisky he managed to spin around on one foot while juggling three lemon-leaf cigars and singing, 'Yo Ho Ho and a Bottle of Rum!' This made all the girl-cats giggle and purr and jiggle from one foot to another so that some of them spilt their drinks and this made them giggle even more. Life at The Cat's Whiskers had never been so much fun before Winnie arrived.

So when our young hero did indeed ask one or another of them to join him on the dancefloor, they were thrilled to bits and all the others felt very envious as they watched their friend being spun around and twirled this way and that as Winnie showed off his rock 'n' roll jiving skills.

All of these young ladies were friendly and very well brought up and the only reason they were allowed to come to The Cat's Whiskers club at all was because they came with their big brothers who kept a watchful eye on them and made sure they went home at a reasonable hour. These big brothers could see that, despite all his showing off, Winnie was a pleasant young man and so they were happy to allow their younger sisters to have fun in his company.

The only trouble was that Winnie was what snuzzles call 'naive'... That's a word which means that he was still very young and trusting and he didn't understand that some moggies might not be quite as nice and honest as they pretended to be. After all, the only ladies he really knew were Hissie and Sylvester who loved him to bits and would never have hurt him for the world. He somehow thought that *all* ladies would be like that.

And if he had kept his attention on those nice well brought-up girls with their friendly big brothers, all would have been well. But Winnie didn't keep his attention on those nice well brought-up girls with their friendly big brothers, oh no...! You see (and you won't be surprised when I tell you this), Winnie was always on the lookout for adventure, for something a little bit more exciting than what was right in front of him.

And so, he had noticed another lady-cat who didn't join in with all the young girls but who stayed in the shadows, watching with a slight smile on her face, tapping her foot lightly on the floor in time with the music. She smoked expensive gold-tipped cigarettes which came in fancy packets and she had a special friend known as T.H. who wore black sunglasses over his green eyes and had very big shoulder muscles and a small red ruby in one of his front teeth. They had never come over and spoken to Winnie but had simply watched quietly from their dark corner and applauded politely at the end of his showy-offy displays.

Winnie was intrigued. Who could they be, he wondered? And, more importantly, who could *she* be...? The air of mystery around this lady had captivated Winnie and he was determined to get to know her better.

So one evening after the other nice young ladies had been taken home by their big brothers, Winnie took a big swig of catnip whisky and went up to the two figures in the corner. To his surprise and delight, the mysterious lady immediately agreed to dance with him and he found that she was an excellent rock 'n' roll partner. She told him that her name was Minnie the Mouser and she introduced him to her friend, T.H., who shook Winnie by the paw and offered him a cigar.

If Winnie had known that the letters T.H. stood for The Hoodlum, he might have been less naive. And if he had noticed that Minnie the Mouser always managed to keep her face in the shadows, he might have thought twice about her. And if he had wondered why it was that all the young ladies and their protective brothers never came close to Minnie or T.H., he might have saved himself a lot of trouble. But he didn't and so, over the course of several evenings at The Cat's Whiskers, he spent more and more time trying to impress Minnie and less time having fun with the youngsters.

This made the young girl-cats very sad because they all adored Winnie but it was going to make Winnie himself sadder still as you will see...

Late one night when almost everybody had gone home, Winnie found himself alone at the bar with Minnie and T.H. Fat Tom was out the back washing glasses and even Big Mamma wasn't around which was a pity because she would have noticed something was up.

The conversation started pleasantly enough but then, all of a sudden, T.H. (whom we'll call The Hoodlum from now on because that is his proper name) prodded Winnie in the ribs and said with a snarl so that Winnie could see the little red ruby in his tooth glinting in the low light, 'You think you're really something special, don't you, *Pal?*' And he pushed Winnie off his bar stool. 'Quite the showman, aren't you? Got all the ladies eating out of your paw, haven't you? Quite the *Man...!*'

Winnie, who was trying to scramble to his feet again, was completely taken aback by his nasty threatening tone. What did he mean? Why was this happening? What had he done wrong? And why wasn't Minnie doing anything about it? – because Minnie the Mouser was sitting on her barstool, as cool as a cucumber, watching the scene with a smile. She was smoking one of her fancy cigarettes and looking directly at Winnie.

'Listen, Winnie' she purred. 'My friend and I have a little proposition for you...'

'Yes,' growled The Hoodlum, 'a proposition.' Then he looked hard into Winnie's startled eyes and snarled, 'If you're brave enough, of course... Because I don't think you're really very brave at all – Minnie and me, we think you're still wet behind the ears... Ain't that right, Minnie?'

And Minnie quietly replied, 'That's right, T.H., we think he's just a baby...'

This was too much for Winnie. Even though he could now see that Minnie the Mouser wasn't very pretty at all and that she was much older than he had originally thought when she was keeping in the shadows, his young pride was hurt by the suggestion that he, Winnie, who had discovered a magic carpet, and who had rescued Myrtle Turtle, and who was the famous Loulou's courageous co-pilot, was *JUST A BABY!* He was braver than anybody! He wasn't afraid of that stupid big twit with his muscly shoulders! He had had plenty of catnip whisky and he was ready to take on anyone!

'Who are you calling a baby?' he snapped, giving The Hoodlum a clip round the ear. 'Is it a fight you're wanting – 'cos I'll give you fight if that's what you want…!'

But just as The Hoodlum pulled back one of his massive paws ready to punch Winnie full in the face, Minnie spoke:

'A fight won't be necessary, Winnie,' she said, blowing out a stream of catnip smoke and stubbing out her fancy cigarette. 'We just want you to prove your courage. That shouldn't be so difficult, should it?'

'Easy!' Winnie said, squaring his shoulders and looking from one to the other. 'Nothing scares me! *Nothing!*'

'Right, then,' Minnie continued. 'Here's what you're gonna do: You're gonna spend the night on your own locked inside Limassol Castle…'

'Is that all?' sneered Winnie. 'That's *nothing!*'

'Nothing, eh?' laughed Minnie in reply.

'*Nothing*, he says!' The Hoodlum chuckled menacingly. 'Just you wait!' And they laughed so loudly that they both had a coughing fit. But then the laughter stopped abruptly and the two older cats pushed their noses into Winnie's face and Minnie continued:

'It might not look like much, Limassol Castle, but the truth is that every cat that has spent the night in there alone has either gone crazy or dropped down stone dead… The place is cursed, you see, with a big old snuzzle curse… And it's full of scary *ghosts* – the scariest ghosts anyone could ever imagine… Yeah, that's wiped the smile off your face hasn't it?'

It was true. Winnie was feeling very uncertain now. The one thing he really was afraid of was ghosts and the truth is that he didn't like being locked inside anywhere, especially not a spooky castle, all on his own, knowing now that all those other cats had gone crazy or dropped down stone dead when they'd tried it...

He wavered for a moment. He thought of his nice cosy bed up on the roof with Hissie and Loulou and Sylvester all snoring around him. He thought of Katie Snuzzle and Slinky Skinky and the magic carpet and dear old Plug, and he wished with all his might he was anywhere but here. Oh, he was such an idiot! All he had to do was say, No thank you, I'm going home now, you're quite right, I *am* a bit of a baby, cheerio!

But his pride was too much for him. It didn't matter that he no longer liked the look of Minnie the Mouser, all that mattered was that he was not going to give in to these bullies. He *would* spend the night in the castle on his own! He *wouldn't* be scared to death by those ghosts! He, Winnie, would show them!

'I'll do it!' he bellowed back at them, straight into their ugly faces. 'Just tell me when, right?!'

'Saturday night,' Minnie the Mouser and The Hoodlum said in unison. 'We'll meet you here at midnight and take you there...'

And with that they slunk off into the night, leaving Winnie all alone and feeling very small. Saturday night... That was only three nights away!

It was a sad and anxious Winnie who staggered home that night. The worst of it was that he had brought the problem on himself and, what's more, he couldn't tell anybody. If he told the grown-ups, he would just be proving to himself and to Minnie and The Hoodlum that he really *was* a baby and a coward. This was one thing he was going to have to sort out on his own.

And he didn't even clamber up on to the roof that night to sleep. Instead, he curled up beside the rolled-up rug in the hall. He didn't hold out much hope but maybe, just maybe, a little of its magic might help him...

And, strangely enough, something happened the next day that did indeed make him think that there might possibly be some hope for him.

You see, it was now three whole weeks since Winnie had started going down to The Cat's Whiskers night after night, and all those late-night burgers and shots of catnip whisky had left him feeling and looking decidedly seedy and rough around the edges. His sparkly eyes were often bloodshot and he was finding it more and more difficult to creep home quietly at the end of his nights of secret shenanigans. He couldn't judge distances as well as he used to and on two or three occasions, when he was launching himself from the tree and back on to the roof, he ended up in an untidy heap all the way back down on the ground and it jolly well hurt. Not only that, but he made such a racket that he was beginning to worry that the others suspected something.

And he was right. It hadn't taken Loulou, Hissie and Sylvester very long to notice the change in their beloved young scallywag. As usual, Loulou was the first one to realise exactly what was going on because, as you already know, Loulou himself had had quite a rambunctious youth and he knew only too well what that smell was on Winnie's breath.

'It's bootleg catnip whisky,' he explained to Hissie and Sylvester one morning while Winnie was snoring his head off like an old codger. 'He's got a taste for catnip whisky and that can mean only one thing – he's discovered The Cat's Whiskers!'

'Oh gosh! Oh golly!' squealed Hissie, burying her face in her paws. 'Oh my goodness gracious me! Loulou we must *do* something! If we're not careful he'll end up like my old Uncle Samuel who fell in with a bad crowd when he was a young moggy and you know what happened to *him*!'

Loulou did indeed know what had happened to Hissie's Uncle Samuel. It was a very sorry tale. He had been a fine upstanding young fellow until somebody had started pouring catnip whisky into his water bowl for a joke. And the joke hadn't been very funny for very long because in next to no time Samuel had been arrested for causing a disturbance and, when he came out of the Cat Clink where he had been locked up for six weeks with dozens of Cattiosi (which is what we call members of the very dangerous Moggy Mafia) he had joined the terrible Growler Gang and he came to a very sticky end one moonless night in a smelly canal.

Hissie was shaking with fright (as usual) and it took Loulou and Sylvester a long time and two cups of catnip tea (which is delicious and safe and nothing like catnip whisky, just in case you were wondering) to reassure her that all would be well.

'But what can we *do*?' Hissie sobbed. 'The Cat's Whiskers is a terrible place, all sorts of great big bullies hang around there – not to mention some rather dubious young *girl-cats...*'

These words brought many memories back to Loulou's mind. He found himself reminiscing about a little too much catnip whisky and some rather pretty young girl-cats whom his own mother had disapproved of. A tiny smile came to the old cat's lips and for a few moments there was a faraway look in his eye as he remembered the fun he had had. And it hadn't done *him* any harm, had it? Here he was now, a well-respected elderly gentleman with a magnificent magic carpet at his command. Surely he would be able to think of a plan that would protect Winnie whilst still allowing him to enjoy his growing-up time.

And the thing that neither Hissie nor Sylvester knew was that Loulou himself was an honorary member of The Cat's Whiskers. Oh yes! Loulou had once spoken up in court to defend Big Mamma when the Cat Cops were threatening to close down the nightclub, saying it was attracting too much riffraff to the neighbourhood. Loulou had given such a good speech all about feline rights and freedom of movement that the judge and jury had allowed Big Mamma to keep her club open, just as long as she didn't let things get *too* out of hand. And she had been so grateful that she had immediately presented Loulou with a lifetime membership and free drinks whenever he wanted them.

In fact, Loulou had only visited The Cat's Whiskers once (just to be polite) and he hated all the loud banging and crashing and wasn't very good at dancing either so he had never returned but he always bowed politely to Big Mamma when they passed in the street and he was sure she would help them out.

'Just you leave it with me, Hissie,' said Loulou. And then, turning to Sylvester who as you know wasn't nearly as much of a scaredy-cat as Hissie was, he added, 'I'm going to pop out for a while. Make another cup of catnip tea for Hissie and make sure that Winnie has some catacetamol and a big bowl of water when he wakes up. The whole problem will be sorted out by the time I get home...'

Winnie was feeling particularly rough when he woke up later and the full horror of his predicament came flooding back into his mind. So he didn't complain when Sylvester made sure he swallowed his two catacetamol tablets with a lot of cool water and then he allowed both Hissie and Sylvester to massage his neck and shoulders and rub ointment into all the bruises he had got from falling out of the tree. Oh, if only he could tell them the truth! Why had he been so *stupid*!

And then when Loulou got home, Winnie saw that he had That Look on his face – the same look he had had when he had been telling Winnie off for chasing Slinky Skinky on the day he had first found the magic carpet. What now? How could things possibly get any worse?!

'Well, young Winnie!' Loulou said with a frown and a laugh at the same time. 'Your secret is out! We know all about your gadding about and we can see that it's not doing you much good...'

'What do you mean?!' Winnie spluttered. Surely Loulou couldn't know about Minnie the Mouser, could he? Winnie really didn't want to look bad in front of Loulou, he didn't want Loulou to know how stupid he'd been. 'What...?' he repeated.

'Shush!' Loulou interrupted him with a twitch of his tail. 'Let me finish... ' Winnie didn't like the look of that twitching tail so he bit his tongue and tried to look as polite and attentive as possible even though he was still full of fear and the after-effects of too much catnip whisky and not enough sleep.

'I've just been having a meeting with an old friend of mine – Big Mamma...!' said Loulou. 'Yes, I thought that might surprise you all! Big Mamma and I go back a long way and we realise that what Winnie needs is some Adventure...'

At the sound of the word Adventure, Winnie's whole demeanour changed. Yes, yes, *yes*, he thought! An adventure was just what he needed. Especially if it involved the magic carpet! Maybe this was a way he could escape from Minnie the Mouser... Ooh, yes! He'd have to make sure he cleaned his cap (it had got a bit dusty and messed-up from all the nights down at the club).

But Loulou was speaking again:

'You won't be going on the magic carpet again until I'm really sure I can trust you...'

'But, *Loulou*...' Winnie squealed in dismay.

'Hush!' came the firm reply. 'I promised you an adventure and you will have one – maybe more than one – so just pipe down and listen: Big Mamma wasn't the only friend I spent time with today. As luck would have it, another life member of The Cat's Whiskers is in town today – our good friend Plug!'

At this name, everybody erupted in smiles – Winnie, Sylvester, Hissie, and Loulou himself.

'Good old Plug!' sighed Hissie and Sylvester in unison. 'Dear Plug, our hero!'

'Our hero indeed,' agreed Loulou. 'He's only in town for two more days before his boat heads back out to sea and this is where Winnie's adventure comes in. Your wish has come true, my lad! You're going to sea as Plug's assistant rat catcher... Plenty of fresh air and exercise, running about after rats and climbing ropes and ladders and masts and things – and as much fresh fish as you can eat. And Plug for company... Now what do you say to that?'

Winnie didn't know *what* to say! This was a miracle! Off to sea with Plug! No Minnie the Mouser! No Hoodlum! Lots of fresh fish and opportunities to show off and see far horizons! It all sounded too good to be true. Maybe sleeping beside the rug really *had* saved him!

But Loulou was speaking again:

'Big Mamma also mentioned to me that you've been showing a little bit too much interest in a certain moggy of dubious reputation – I won't call her a *lady*-cat... I'm sure you know who I mean...'

At these words, Winnie blushed (which is a difficult thing for a moggy to do but, believe me, you could see his bright pink cheeks all the way through his sleek grey fur). How much did Loulou know? Surely he couldn't know everything? He felt ashamed as he thought of the times he had let Minnie wear his co-pilot's cap. And he felt even worse when he remembered that he had thought she looked very attractive with it pulled down over one eye. The cap had seemed to go perfectly with her stockings, which were made of real fishnet, and her high heels decorated with tiny pearls, given to her over the years by her many admirers from the oyster-collecting ships. (Just in case you didn't know, pearls are found inside oysters.)

'Yes,' said Loulou, 'I can see from your red face that you know who I'm talking about. It's quite obvious you've become far too keen on her and so I'm going to put some distance between you for a fortnight so you can come to your senses...'

Wow! thought Winnie, I *have* been rescued! For two whole weeks I'll be far far away, out at sea! Surely, Minnie and the Hoodlum can't touch me there! And Loulou thinks I still *like* her which means he doesn't know about the Dare to stay in the Castle all alone overnight... Better and better! And he did a somersault which Loulou found very perplexing. After all, he had just told this young whippersnapper that

he was being sent off to sea, far away from the girl
he was showing such interest in, and here he was doing
somersaults... Very odd. *Very* odd indeed.

But Loulou had got so used to Winnie being odd that he
put it out of his mind. It was just Winnie being Winnie.

The next two days were a whirl of activity. There were so
many things to organise to get Winnie ready for his first stint
as Plug's assistant at sea.

Hissie knitted him a navy blue fisherman's jersey with
a big white fish on the front because, even though
it was still summertime, she knew that as soon as
the weather changed towards autumn it would get
very cold at night out there on the water and she didn't
want to take any chances with her beloved Winnie. She
also carefully cleaned and repaired his smart co-pilot's
cap which had been shamefully bashed about during his
secret visits to The Cat's Whiskers.

And Loulou had a few words to say about *that* too:

'Now listen very carefully, Winnie,' he said while Sylvester and Hissie were busy
squeezing everything he would need into his new backpack. 'You're to do everything
that Plug tells you, understand? The sea can be a dangerous place as you've already
discovered – and it will be particularly dangerous because you won't have me and the
magic carpet with you. We can't have any of your clowning about, OK?'

Winnie – who had been planning on doing a lot of clowning about – crossed his
paws behind his back and said, 'Yes, Loulou, I'll be good...'

'I somehow doubt that,' said Loulou with a sigh, 'but I do want you to try. I know
you think that Sylvester and Hissie and I are just old fuddy-duddies
who want to spoil your fun, but nothing could be further from the
truth. We just want to keep you safe because...' he hesitated for a
moment and then continued, '... because we love you very much...'

Winnie felt himself starting to blush all over again. Loulou
had never said anything like that before and it made
him feel rather guilty that he had crossed his paws
behind his back when promising to be good.

'Now there's something very important I need to
tell you now,' Loulou went on. 'Listen very carefully
and remember what I'm going to say because it could
save your life one day... '

He was looking directly into Winnie's eyes with an extremely intense expression so Winnie sat up very straight and pricked up his ears. This sounded serious.

'You may have noticed that I wasn't at home last night,' Loulou said.

'Yes, I did wonder where you'd gone,' said Winnie with his head on one side because it had indeed puzzled him, 'but I was so tired after trying to decide all the things I needed to take in my backpack that I fell asleep and then in the morning there you were again just like normal.'

'Quite,' said Loulou, 'just like normal... Except *not* just like normal... You see, I had to take a solo trip on the magic carpet...'

'What!' exclaimed Winnie in dismay. 'You went on the magic carpet without *me*! – without your co-pilot!'

'I had no choice, Winnie,' said Loulou, hiding a smile at the young rascal's indignation. 'It was a trip I had to take for your benefit. Let me explain: You remember the story of how the magic carpet came to be and of how every thread and every stitch has magic in it and of how it is I, Loulou, and I alone who can give the carpet orders?'

Winnie nodded his head. 'Yes, Loulou, of course I remember,' he said politely, wishing that Loulou would get on with the story about where he had been last night.

'Well,' said Loulou, 'even though I can give the carpet instructions, there are certain things that I have to be given permission to do. I had to travel through the different dimensions to The Unnamed Planet which is where Shentoro is now living. You remember who Shentoro is, don't you?'

Winnie nodded his head very very fast. 'Yes, Loulou, he's the wizard you helped hundreds of years ago when your name was Derrashah and you were on the planet Zennadon......'

'Quite right,' agreed Loulou. 'Well, I had to go and ask his permission to take one single thread from the magic carpet so that Hissie could stitch it very carefully and cleverly inside *this*...!'

And as he said these words, he pulled out Winnie's smart co-pilot's cap from behind his back with a flourish. 'Look here!' he said. 'You see these tiny golden stitches under the rim at the back – well, tucked away behind them is one single magic thread from the carpet and, when you're in really big trouble you must put your paw on those stitches and call my name. The minute you do that I'll hear you and I *may* be able to do something to help you.'

'Wow!' gasped Winnie. 'You mean I've got a magic cap all of my own!'

'Yes and no...' Loulou replied. 'Your co-pilot's cap is very important. It's a great honour to have it and it's not something to get all messed up and covered in catnip beer at The Cat's Whiskers, do you understand?'

Winnie hung his head and muttered, 'Yes, Loulou, I do understand, I'm sorry...'

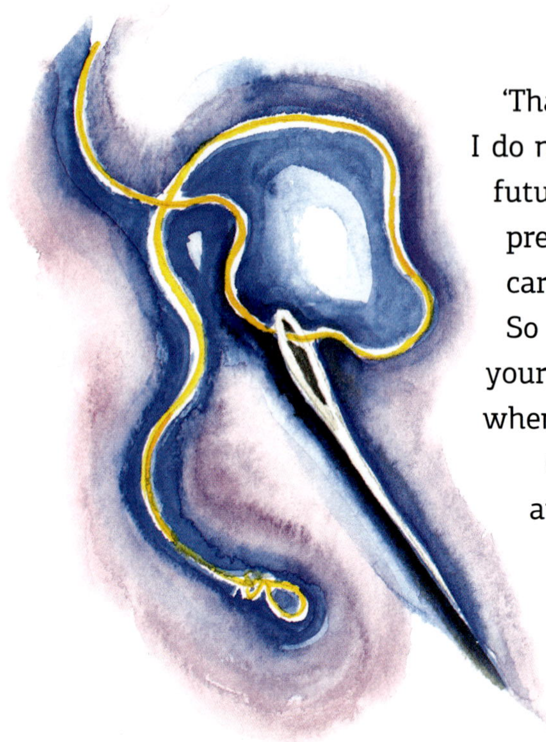

'That's all right,' said Loulou kindly, 'I'm not cross but I do need you to understand and look after it properly in future. You see, although it isn't magic itself, that one precious thread from the carpet which Hissie has so carefully and lovingly stitched inside for you *is* magic. So it's very important that you always know where your cap is so you can easily touch those magical stitches when you need to... Understood?'

Once again Winnie nodded his head very vigorously up and down and Loulou continued with his explanation: 'The thing is, young Winnie, the thread will only respond when you are in Serious Trouble – *not* when you're just in one of your silly scrapes! You can't go taking risks every five minutes because you think all you have to do is touch the stitches and Loulou will come zooming in on the magic carpet! It doesn't work like that! It's what we call "an avenue of last resort" – something you can turn to when all else fails. It's not a toy but it's there to let me know when your life is in danger. It still doesn't mean I can necessarily get to you in time but it does mean we have a chance and I will always do whatever I can to protect you.'

Winnie was beginning to feel rather sombre by this time and that is exactly what Loulou wanted him to feel. He didn't want to spoil the young scamp's fun but he did need him to understand that going to sea with Plug required him to start behaving a bit more like a grown-up and not to take too many silly risks.

'Remember, Winnie,' Loulou added, 'as I've told you before, I know very well what it's like to be young and headstrong and I want you to enjoy every moment of every adventure. I had plenty of narrow escapes myself when I was your age – maybe one day I'll tell you about them – but while you're away it's going to seem very quiet around Malekidi Street and we're all going to miss you very much and we want to be sure that you come home safe and sound to tell us all about your travels.'

And Loulou put his big black paw around Winnie's shoulder and gave him a hug. And he repeated the magic words which brought a big shiny tear to Winnie's eye, 'We all love you very much – and we are very proud of you too. You're a good, brave boy...'

That night as Winnie stretched out under the stars on the roof, listening to Loulou and Hissie and Sylvester snoring gently beside him, he felt a great warmth in his heart as it beat in his chest.

'Yes,' he said to himself, 'I understand now, they really do love me. And I love them too.' And all in a big rush he realised how much he was going to miss them – much more than he could ever have missed Minnie the Mouser, even in the days when he had thought she was so marvellous – and he thought to himself, 'This must be what it's like to grow up a bit... You realise how much you love people...'

And he fell asleep a little bit older and wiser than he had been five minutes before.

The next day everything happened very quickly. Hissie made sure he ate a big breakfast and then Plug came round to doublecheck the contents of his backpack and presented him with his very own compass so that if he ever got shipwrecked he would know which direction was north (which Winnie didn't think would be much help to him really but he still felt proud of having such a grown-up gadget). Sylvester insisted on giving him one final swimming lesson in the water butt and Loulou placed his special cap on his head.

'There!' he said. 'Now you look magnificent! Have a wonderful time and we'll all see you in two weeks when Plug brings you back to us for a little holiday. The only problem is that Katie Snuzzle is bound to worry about you – she'll wonder where you've gone. We'll do our best to keep her mind on other things and, after the first few times you've been away and then come back safely, she'll have got used to it and not worry so much. But you *must* make an extra big fuss of her and be on your best behaviour when you do come home, OK? You know what snuzzles are like, they need to feel appreciated, and it's a big part of our job to make sure they do...'

And so it was that, with Hissie trying not to burst into tears, and with Loulou and Sylvester waving their paws in the air, Winnie and Plug set off down the street in the direction of the harbour.

Winnie's heart was as light as a feather. He had been saved! Nothing could touch him now, not ever!

Or so he thought...

Because, you see, being sent away as Plug's assistant was what is known as a reprieve – which is *not* the same as being rescued. A reprieve is only for a little while. He wasn't out of danger yet. Oh no! Minnie the Mouser and The Hoodlum weren't going to let him get away *that* easily!

It felt so good out there, leaning forwards over the waves

66

5

A LIFE ON THE OCEAN WAVE

For the next six months Winnie's life was like a jigsaw puzzle with all sorts of colourful and differently shaped pieces slotting in together. For two weeks he would be a busy ship's cat, every day different from the one before, depending on the wind and the weather, and sometimes he was so tired from all the work he had to do that he became quite dizzy and cross-eyed. And then for the next two weeks he would be at home in Malekidi Street, sleeping as long as he liked and telling Loulou all about his adventures and being spoiled rotten by Hissie and Sylvester. And the only thing that was the same about the two weeks when he was on the boat and the two weeks when he was at home was that he never stopped showing off. Somehow, Winnie and showing off went together like bread and jam.

But what about Minnie the Mouser, I hear you ask? What about The Hoodlum and the Dare and the night all alone in the Castle? What about all *that*?!

Well, perhaps a little of the carpet's magic had indeed rubbed off on Winnie because his reprieve went on a bit longer than any of us could have expected. You see, Minnie and The Hoodlum were a thoroughly bad lot so they were always up to no good, stealing things and beating moggies up and scratching snuzzles' ankles just for fun. And all this bad behaviour meant that the Cat Cops had had their eye on the dynamic duo for ages but had never been able to arrest them because Minnie and The Hoodlum were too quick and too clever.

67

However, one night, just after Winnie had gone off to sea for the first time, their luck finally ran out.

The Cops had been tipped off that the two crooks were going to carry out a daring robbery at the very posh house of Persian Pete, an extremely pampered puss who had a diamond collar. It was this diamond collar that Minnie so wanted and it was her greed that made her careless.

As soon as Persian Pete had eaten his dinner (into which The Hoodlum had poured a huge dose of valerian and catnip sleeping potion), he naturally fell into a deep sleep and Minnie quickly unbuckled the magnificent collar, her eyes bright with greedy triumph. But then, instead of scarpering straight away as they had agreed they would, she couldn't resist putting the collar around her own slender neck and gazing at her reflection in the hall mirror of the big house where Persian Pete and his wealthy snuzzle lived.

And those extra two minutes gave the Cat Cops the opportunity they needed, so that before Minnie and The Hoodlum knew what was happening, they were surrounded by six big whiskery police-mogs and the game was up.

'Caught red-handed!' cried the Top Cop, as he whisked away the diamond-studded collar and replaced it round the big fluffy neck of Persian Pete who was still out for the count, completely unaware of all the kerfuffle going on around him.

'Six months in the Cat Clink Prison!' announced the judge as soon as the cops had dragged Minnie and The Hoodlum to the cat-courthouse, which was set up under a big tree in the garden of the snuzzles' own Court House in Lord Byron Avenue.

'Six months!' the judge repeated. 'And next time it will be much longer! I hope you've learnt your lesson!'

Well, you can imagine how relieved and excited Winnie was when he heard this news as he arrived home with Plug after his first two-week stint on the boat.

'Saved!' he squealed in delight. 'I really am saved! Six months in the Cat Clink Prison! Six months is for ever...!'

Only, of course, you and I know very well that six months is NOT for ever. In fact, it's not very long at all – especially when you're having fun and time is whizzing by and you're making the most of every single minute...

But Winnie felt his happiness was now complete and so the next six months were, in his own words, 'ABSOLUTELY FAN-TAS-TIC!' (And by the time he had said this on at least 38 different occasions, even his devoted Auntie Hissie was a bit fed up with it.)

But the main thing was that Winnie was deliriously happy.

The best thing about being on the fishing boat was that everything was New and Different. He had explored every nook and cranny of Number 9 Malekidi Street so it held very few surprises for him but here on the boat there was nothing *but* surprises

– some good, some bad, but all of them super-interesting. For a start, there was the motion of the boat itself. Even the slightest swell on the sea made the decks and walkways dance under Winnie's feet and, as if that weren't enough, they were often wet with slippery seawater so that he slid about all over the place and sometimes ended up flat on his back, sliding this way and that, much to the amusement of Plug and the three fishermen on board – the brothers Panos, Yiannos and Phanos, who all worked very hard and always smelt of fish which Winnie found very pleasant.

When Plug first introduced Winnie as his new assistant to the three brothers, they were all very welcoming and gave him some prawns for his first dinner on board.

'That's a great honour,' said Plug as Winnie tucked in. 'Make sure you do your job well or else they'll put you on short rations – especially Panos, he can be quite a slave driver. He's the muscly one with the long pigtail and the pinky-red t-shirt. The others tease him about his long hair, telling him it's "girly", but trust me, Winnie, there's nothing girly about him! I call him Mr Macho and I make sure I never tread on his toes!'

For the first few days Winnie was so busy he didn't know whether he was up or down or here or there. One minute he was catching mice and the next he was having fisticuffs with Hercules, the biggest rat he had ever seen and whom Plug respected, even though he was such a terror on the boat. Then he would be busily cleaning Plug's sleeping quarters (an extra big bunk with a plush red towel inside) and several times a day he had to shin up the mast to chat with Walter, the friendly chief seagull who told them where the fish were congregating. Winnie would then pass this information to Plug who would then go and tell the fishermen so they had the best chance of getting a good catch.

It goes without saying that Winnie got into plenty of scrapes and had more mishaps than I can tell you about here. For example, he got so badly tangled up in the nets one morning that he would have got thrown overboard if Plug hadn't happened to come along at just the right moment. And there were several occasions when stormy weather gave him such terrible seasickness that his grey coat turned green and his eyes went yellow. He was not a pretty sight.

'Don't worry,' said Plug reassuringly. 'You'll soon get used to it!'

Winnie felt so ill that he didn't believe him at first but surprise, surprise, it turned out to be true. After the first two or three storms, something changed inside him, as if a switch had been turned on, so that, not only did he stop being seasick, but he quickly started to enjoy the wild weather. In fact, the wilder the better. When the wind blew and the waves reared up all around the boat, it felt crazy and exciting – just like Winnie himself – so that, by the end of his third stint at sea, he was longing for a good old squall so that he could go skittering along the decks and up the mast and hang on for dear life as the boat dipped and tossed in the churning green water.

Then there was the dreadful time he got a fish bone stuck in his throat when he was being greedy at supper. Nothing would budge it and in the end he had to put up with a very uncomfortable shipboard operation in which Panos and Yiannos (who were the biggest) held him down flat on his back while Phanos (who was the one with the fishiest fingers), prised his mouth wide open and Plug hooked the bone out with his long claw.

That was one experience Winnie never wanted to repeat and from then on he took great care when fish was on the menu (which of course was every day when they were on the boat).

And even though the boat only stayed out at sea for 48 hours at a time, Winnie and Plug had to stay on board, or close at hand, while all the fish were being offloaded and taken to market. Their work contract stated that they must work full-time for two whole weeks and then they would have two whole weeks ashore.

During these times, Plug would go and stay with his sister Molly while Winnie would bask in the luxury of the big wicker basket with his own special quilt which Katie Snuzzle had prepared for him and which Hissie and Sylvester kept warm for him while he was away. The reason that Katie Snuzzle had gone to the trouble of getting this plush basket especially for young Winnie was that, when he disappeared for his first two weeks with Plug, she had no idea where he had gone and she was so thrilled when he returned safely that she bought it for him as a Welcome Home present. And then, just as Loulou had predicted, she gradually got used to the fact that he was at home for a little while and would then disappear but always come back, so everyone was happy.

Winnie loved his holidays back in Malekidi Street. Loulou had once told him a story about a little boy-snuzzle who had gone away to boarding school all the way across the sea in England and this little boy was so happy to travel home for the school holidays because there was no work for him to do and there were loads of treats and lots of fun to be had. The little boy-snuzzle called the school holidays 'the Hols' and so this is what Winnie called them too. 'I'm going home for the Hols tomorrow!' he would say at the end of a busy two weeks on board the *Oi Tharalea Thalessea Gata* (which in future I will call by its English name *The Courageous Sea-Cat* because that's much easier to remember). And 'I wish the Hols could go on for ever!' he would sigh as he tucked into one of Hissie's mouse-and-moth pies, which were a speciality of hers. He even looked forward to seeing Slinky Skinky again and, even though he still chased him all around the garden and up the lemon tree, they both remembered how they had shared in the discovery of the magic carpet and that made them feel like brothers (not very *friendly* brothers, perhaps, but brothers nevertheless).

Another feature of the Hols was that Winnie was able to visit The Cat's Whiskers again, which was something he could enjoy to the full since he knew that Minnie the Mouser and The Hoodlum were safely behind bars. However, Loulou insisted that he only went there in the company of Plug. And there was to be no catnip whisky, just catnip beer which was much safer for a young lad. And Big Mamma promised Loulou that she and Fat Tom the barman would keep an eye on the young chap, just to be on the safe side. And Plug was always very kind because he remembered what it was like to be young and skittish and so he would often go inside to play Chinese Checkers with his Siamese friend Hing Fing Ping, leaving Winnie free to lark about on the dancefloor and indulge in his usual showing off in front of the nice young girl-cats with their big brothers.

And then, all too soon, the Hols would be over and Plug and Winnie would be packing their backpacks and once again clambering back aboard *The Courageous Sea-Cat.*

And often, as he lay in his gently swaying hammock on that first night away from home again, Winnie would find himself shedding tears of homesickness, just as the little boy-snuzzle had done on his first night back at boarding school in the story that Loulou had told him. But the sadness never lasted long and before you could say

Miggy-Moggy-Moo he was once again sliding along the slippery decks and teasing Walter the seagull and catching dozens of mice so that Yiannos, Panos and Phanos would praise him to the heavens and tell him he was the cleverest cat that Cyprus had ever produced. But he never managed to catch Hercules, the biggest toughest rat, and that was the only thing that made him cross.

Back home, he had never paid much attention to the weather. He loved the sunshine and leaping about in the garden after butterflies and then, when the wind and the rain came, he would simply go inside for a snooze. But here on the boat it was a very different story and he came to love every single kind of weather there was.

He loved the excitement of a strong wind and he would tear up the mast and cling on for dear life as the boat tossed this way and that and his ears and whiskers got blown so far backwards that he felt sure they must come off. And sometimes (when Plug wasn't looking because this really was extremely dangerous) he would rush to the very front of the boat, dig his claws in as much as he could and lean right out over the prow just as he had seen somebody do on a DVD called 'Titanic' which Katie Snuzzle had been watching one evening when Winnie was still a kitten and curled up on her knee. Ooh, it felt so *good* out there, leaning forwards over the waves and getting windblown and splashed with salty water! – until the time when an enormous wave splashed right up into his face and he lost his grip and was swept all the way back to the other end of the boat, bumping into crates and nets and lobster pots and other sticky-up things as he went, so that by the time he came to rest in the far corner he was so battered and bruised he felt as if he had been in a big battle (and, as he was soon to discover, a real big battle was not that far away, the Biggest Adventure of his life so far was looming towards him...)

On other days when it was sunny and warm and the water was like glass and the boat was at anchor and everyone was feeling lazy, then Plug and Winnie would slip silently over the side wearing their special snorkels which a friend of Plug's had made for them. They would try to catch the little silvery fish which darted this way and that in the crystal clear water and sometimes they dived down and tugged at the sea anemones' tentacles which tickled them and made them laugh. And at those times, Winnie wished that Sylvester could have been there because she so loved swimming and it seemed unfair that she only had the water butt to splash about in and he had the whole of the Mediterranean Sea. He was the luckiest boy-cat in the world!

On cold days and nights he had Hissie's lovely warm jumper to snuggle in and of course he always kept his co-pilot's cap with its magic thread close at hand just in case (which, as you will soon see, was just as well...)

The weeks and months flew by. Winnie's world was so full of new experiences and sounds and smells and tastes that he often felt he was inside a huge spinning top, whirling round and round, surrounded by bright colours and wild music and a sort of whooshing sound that made his ears and whiskers quiver with excitement.

It wasn't only the beautiful boat that was full of interesting surprises and games but also the port where Yiannos, Panos and Phanos docked the boat every couple of days so they could go and sell their catch at the fish market. After Plug and Winnie had completed their chores on board so that everything was 'shipshape and Bristol fashion', they would set off for the working cats' club inside an old wrecked ship which had been abandoned and left to rot and where no snuzzles ever came.

This was a very different place from The Cat's Whiskers but every bit as much fun in its own way:

There was sawdust on the floor and a thick haze of catnip-tobacco smoke which made Winnie's eyes water. Plug didn't approve of smoking and he was constantly telling Winnie that if he wanted the girls to like him he would be much better off saying 'No thank you' if anyone ever offered him what he called a Sickarette ('because it'll make you sick, see?').

'It'll make your whiskers all yellow and smelly and you don't want that now do you?'

'No!' said Winnie, who was rather a vain young fellow and certainly didn't want his good-looking face to be spoilt by smelly yellow whiskers.

Still, despite the haze of catnip-tobacco smoke in the club, Winnie loved the place and so did Plug. For one thing it was crammed with interesting foreigners. They came off the boats and the big ships and the container vessels from every corner of the world and they spoke all sorts of different languages but somehow managed to make themselves understood so everyone had a good time. Mind you, there were occasions when 'a good time' meant an energetic rough-and-tumble with lots of fur flying here and there. But nobody ever got seriously hurt, just duffed-up a bit which Winnie found quite exciting to watch, although he stuck close to Plug at these times and managed to keep out of trouble.

There were football matches, using old ping-pong balls, and there was a dart board made out of an old chocolate box; and some of the Chinese cats taught Winnie and Plug how to play a Chinese game called Miaow Jong which involved pushing small tiles made of mouse bones around the floor in a special sequence which Winnie could never quite understand.

There were also some enormous Russian cats who had big square heads and were very good at wrestling, and another crew of Siamese cats who set up a kitchen in the club where they cooked huge pots of spicy fish heads with seaweed which was everybody's favourite so the Siamese cats were very popular. They were friends of Plug's special pal Hing Fing Ping and were called Hong, Fong and Pong (although nobody could ever remember which was which and who was who).

But the one member of the working cats' club who fascinated Winnie the most was a very old and very skinny Indian cat who did marvellous tricks. He was called Mog Dahl and he had a big crate of spiny spiky sea urchins, as sharp as needles, and he could stretch out on his back on top of all those spiny spikes and not get hurt at all even though his coat and his skin were so thin. He said it was all because of the power of his mind and he challenged everyone to try it for themselves but nobody else could do it, not even Plug, and Winnie decided not to try.

Winnie spent hours with Mog Dahl, listening to stories of cat-gods with three heads and dozens of arms, who lived in the Himalayas. And Mog Dahl taught Winnie how to breathe through one nostril at a time and how to stare at a snake so it wouldn't bite him (which Winnie would later discover was a very useful thing to be able to do).

And then one day, right out of the blue, the old Indian cat called everyone around him and said it was time for him to say Goodbye, because he was going off to another planet.

Well, of course, nobody believed him –

except Winnie, who trusted Mog Dahl completely and who believed in magical things because he knew that Loulou had lived for thousands of years and had spent a lot of time with Shentoro the wizard on the Planet Zennadon.

So Winnie was the only one who wasn't surprised by what happened next. They all trooped outside and the old Indian cat settled himself down on a pile of coiled rope and closed his eyes and started to hum a mystical mysterious hum. 'Hum-um-um-um...' he intoned as he started to sway gently to and fro and back and forth. And then, smoothly and silently, all by itself, the coil of rope began to uncoil itself, gradually straightening up, up, up into the night sky, higher and higher, until it was completely straight and Mog Dahl was right up at the very top, still sitting there, still humming, still the same as ever. And then suddenly, *whoosh*, he was gone... just like that... in a puff of smoke... right up there into the sky... *Gone!* And everybody who was there that night will remember that moment for ever.

So, as you can see, Winnie's life was a magical world of excitement. But the very best thing of all during that first six months was what happened on his first Christmas at sea. It was like nothing he could ever have imagined...

The Christmas celebrations started off at lunchtime with a big bang. Yiannos, Panos and Phanos opened a bottle of Cyprus brandy and, as they had done every Christmas Eve for as long as Plug could remember, the three fishermen added a little of this delicious but very alcoholic drink to the water bowls of their moggy friends. Being an old sea-cat himself, Plug was used to this and of course Winnie had had plenty of practice in his early days of swigging the bootleg catnip whisky at The Cat's Whiskers, but Cyprus brandy is very strong and Winnie soon felt squiffy and had to roll off down to his cabin for a couple of hours' kip in his hammock.

When he woke up, it was quite dark and he could hear loud singing and laughter coming from up above.

'How are you feeling now, son?' came Plug's voice from his comfortable bunk. 'I finished my drink just to be polite even though I don't really like the stuff – I much prefer the good old catnip beer, much better for us cats. Have you got a sore head?'

'Not really,' said Winnie. 'But I had some very strange dreams while I was asleep...' He yawned loudly and stretched. 'So what happens now?' he asked. 'What happens at Christmas on a boat?'

'Well,' said Plug, chewing thoughtfully on his piece of catnip tobacco. 'In about an hour, we'll go back upstairs and have our dinner with the snuzzles – but don't worry, they won't give you any more brandy. They might be very drunk themselves but they never forget that you and I are here to work and we need to keep a clear head...'

'Is that all?' Winnie said in a small and rather disappointed voice. 'We have our dinner every night with Panos and Yiannos and Phanos so what makes tonight different?'

'You'll see,' said Plug mysteriously. 'You'll just have to wait and see.'

A couple of hours later Winnie had to admit to himself that he was still a bit disappointed. True, he'd enjoyed having extra delicious rations (fresh mussels and some swordfish steak) and he'd also enjoyed the way that the fishermen had picked him up and tickled his tummy and let him walk about all over the makeshift table eating the leftovers from their own plates (he'd never tasted fried onions and garlic bread before but decided he liked them). But still, he couldn't say it was really *that* exciting...

'Right then,' Plug suddenly announced, arching his back and hopping down from the table. 'Time for us to get back down below...'

What?! thought Winnie, surely it wasn't bedtime already! They hadn't done *anything* yet, not really...

But Plug was striding purposefully in the direction of their sleeping quarters below decks, leaving the three sozzled snuzzles slumped in their seats, singing sentimental songs and hiccuping comfortably to themselves. Oh well, Winnie thought, never mind, I'm sure that Hissie and Sylvester and Loulou will have something special in mind for Christmas when I go home in a couple of days. And he trotted on after Plug feeling rather disconsolate (a big word which means 'down in the dumps').

But what was all *this*?!

Winnie couldn't believe his eyes...

As he followed Plug into their sleeping quarters beside the lifeboat, the first thing he noticed was that the whole place was festooned with the twinkliest little lights he had ever seen. It was like fairyland or one of those other magic places he had heard Loulou talking about and, on closer inspection, he saw that every single little light was actually a tiny dancing firefly. And not only were these fireflies dancing but they were singing as well – a happy, friendly sound which made his own heart sing. And, even though he knew that fireflies came in the summer not at Christmas, there was such a feeling of magic in the air that it seemed the most natural thing in the world to discover that his dark sleeping quarters had been transformed into a Christmas Wonderland.

Festooned all around the room were streamers made of feathery seaweed which had been dried and dipped in silver paint so that they sparkled in the light of the fireflies; and, laid out on a tray made from oyster shells, there were two crystal glasses filled to the brim with something bubbly and pink. And in front of the glasses there was an enormous Christmas card made from a piece of very thin, very white driftwood, sprinkled with glittery sand and with the words 'To Our Very Good Friends Plug and Winnie!' in big red letters on the front. And on the back were the words, 'We Wish You a Very Merry Christmas and We'll See You at Midnight!'

And all of a sudden Winnie's low spirits had flown all the way up as far as they could go and he was jumping up and down in the highest of high spirits imaginable.

'Who is it *from*?!' he squealed. '*Who*'s coming at midnight?! And who put all these lovely fireflies everywhere? – and the streamers and that lovely-looking drink that's full of bubbles...?!'

He was dancing from foot to foot all in a tizzy and Plug was laughing so hard that he had to lie down in his bunk because his tummy was hurting and his legs felt weak.

Once he had recovered and was able to speak, he said:

'It's half-past-eleven now so you've only got half an hour to wait. Trust me, you're going to see something you've never seen before and it's going to change your life!'

At these words, Winnie became almost beside himself, spinning around like a top and bouncing off the walls like a squash ball. Something that was going to change his life! What on earth could that be? And he still didn't understand where all the Christmas decorations had come from. He knew that Plug couldn't have done it because Plug had been up top with him ever since they had left their sleeping quarters two hours ago. How could he possibly be expected to wait a whole 30 minutes? It really wasn't fair!

'Maybe *this* will help to pass the time,' Plug said kindly, holding out a small parcel wrapped in Christmas paper. 'I hope you like it,' he added almost shyly. 'I had one of these when I was a lad and I really loved it – I learnt to do all sorts of fancy tricks with it. Go on then, open it...'

Winnie quickly cut through the paper with his sharp claws and there in his paw was a shiny bright red yo-yo.

'Oh, Plug! Thank you so much, I've never tried one of these... I don't even know what it is! Please show me!'

And so for the next half-hour Plug taught Winnie how to play with the yo-yo and the old sea-cat discovered that he hadn't forgotten how to do all those tricks from his youth so, just for once, it was Plug rather than Winnie who was enjoying showing off. Winnie was completely captivated by all the clever things Plug could do with this simple little yo-yo and he'd already decided he was going to impress everybody down at The Cat's Whiskers with his skill. It was such fun that the half-hour went by in a flash and all of a sudden Winnie heard an unfamiliar sound coming closer and closer to where he and Plug were sitting side-by-side on Plug's bunk.

Plug but his paw to his lips and whispered, 'Sshhh, now, and listen... Happy Christmas, Winnie, this is what we've been waiting for...'

And Winnie listened very hard and gradually he recognised the tune of a snuzzle Christmas Carol: 'Silent night, Holy night, All is calm, All is bright...'

And, as the humming and singing grew louder, his eyes turned to the doorway in utter amazement as a huge stream of creatures began to flood into the room. At the front came Hercules the enormous rat and he was followed by one... two... three... 10... 25... 100... TWO HUNDRED mice! Winnie couldn't believe his eyes! Two hundred mice! And they were still coming, more and more and more! And rats too, not just Hercules... And a swarm of cockroaches! Oh my goodness! And lizards and beetles of every size and colour... What was this? – Noah's Ark?

And every single one of them was humming and singing that lovely tune, the snuzzle Christmas song 'Silent Night'. And they were carrying little firefly lanterns and smiling. Winnie was spellbound, he couldn't understand why he didn't want to pounce on any of them, he was in a sort of trance. It was all so beautiful, the sounds and the lights and all the little (and some not so little) creatures filling up the whole of the sleeping quarters.

And then quite suddenly everything went quiet and Winnie watched in amazement as Plug and the massive rat Hercules walked towards each other and stood in the middle of the circle and touched noses. Then Plug picked up one of the two crystal glasses from the oyster shell tray and handed it to Hercules and then picked up the other one for himself and together they raised their glasses and said in unison, 'A very Merry Christmas everyone!' And Winnie found himself joining in with all the little mouse and lizard and beetle voices: 'A very Merry Christmas everyone!'

And the next thing was that a stout lady rat (whose name was Gloria) came through the door pushing a trolley made out of an old skate board, on which there were hundreds of little crystal glasses all filled with the magical bubbly liquid. 'Help yourselves everybody!' she cried. 'There's plenty to go round!'

Winnie's eyes were out on stalks. Several mice and too many beetles to count had scuttled up to him to wish him a Happy Christmas and compliment him on his fisherman's jersey and co-pilot's cap. They couldn't have been friendlier and he felt all warm and fuzzy inside. Was he dreaming? Had he had more of that Cyprus brandy then he realised? And where was Plug?

He looked around, craning his long neck over the throng of creatures swirling about wishing each other all good things and occasionally breaking into song or doing a few dance steps – which is quite complicated when you have six legs as was the case with the beetles and cockroaches. Ah, there he was! – deep in conversation with Hercules and Gloria.

Plug turned towards Winnie and grinned. 'Come and join us,' he said, raising his glass. 'I'm about to make my speech and I want you to be right at the front.'

So, with his little glass refilled with the delicious bubbly liquid (which was raspberry champagne, provided by the mice who had had it shipped over specially from a particular field in the South of France), Winnie sat down at Plug's feet, surrounded by all his new and extremely unusual friends, and waited till the hubbub had died down and all was quiet. And then Plug spoke:

'My dear friends, old and new – some of whom I have met time and again and others who are new to our gathering tonight – I want to introduce you to a very special young friend of mine, Winnie…'

And all the voices cried out together, 'Hello Winnie! Happy Christmas!'

And Winnie blushed from the tip of his nose to the tip of his tail and replied, 'And a very happy Christmas to you, too!'

'Winnie is my new comrade on board the *The Courageous Sea-Cat* and I know that some of you have met him already!' And they all laughed as they remembered how they had just managed to escape from Winnie's claws and jaws over the few months since he had been on the boat.

'Yes, some of you have had some narrow escapes – from Winnie as well as from me – and of course some of your friends weren't so lucky…' And a murmur rippled through the crowd as they remembered their loved ones who had lost their lives as Winnie and Plug were doing their duty of keeping the boat free of rats and mice and other unwelcome visitors.

'Now, Winnie,' Plug continued, 'I owe you an explanation. In fact, we all owe you an explanation so just listen carefully while I make everything clear to you. This is a story for you to remember so you can pass it on to your children and your children's children:

'Over 100 years ago there was a terrible war amongst the snuzzles. It was truly awful and millions of snuzzles were killed – all for very stupid reasons that aren't worth telling you about. And it wasn't only snuzzles who died in that awful war but millions and zillions of horses and donkeys and dogs and moggies and rats and mice and every kind of animal you can think of.

'And then, on Christmas Eve 1914 a single brown rat decided to do something extraordinary. He came out of his safe hiding place in the German trenches (the Germans were on one side in the Snuzzle War) and he walked all the way across to where the British enemy were waiting (the British were on the other side in the Snuzzle War). Then he walked straight up to a scraggy moggy who had found himself caught up amongst the enemy army and he touched that scraggy moggy very gently on the nose with his own little snout as a sign of friendship and Christmas spirit. And

the two animals put their arms around each other and walked into the very middle
of the space that separated the two armies.

'And then a wonderful thing happened:

'One of the German soldier-snuzzles was so impressed by what these two animals
had done – two animals, a rat and a cat, who are supposed to be sworn enemies –
that he decided to follow their example. He walked right out into the middle of the
space between the two armies (a piece of land which is called No Man's Land) and
he started singing that lovely snuzzle Christmas song "Silent Night" and continued
walking towards the enemy on the other side. And would you believe it?! – the
snuzzle-soldiers on the British side all started to join in until the night sky in that
terrible place was filled with the sound of snuzzle voices singing and wishing each
other happy Christmas and offering each other good things to drink...

'They all knew that it wouldn't be long before they had to start fighting each other
again – even though they all also knew what a stupid, *stupid* thing that was – but
for those few short hours they were not enemies any more but just ordinary snuzzles
sharing their stories and their friendship with other ordinary snuzzles.

'And the cat and the rat who had started the whole thing told the story to their own
friends and families and they all decided that, whenever it was possible and especially

when they found themselves in any kind of battle – just like the battle between us sea-cats and you shipboard rodents and beetles – they would on Christmas Eve at midnight forget that they were supposed to be enemies and spend a few magical hours in a spirit of friendship and kindness...'

Plug's voice sounded husky now and most of the creatures in the silent room had tears rolling down their cheeks as they nodded their heads and embraced their neighbours. And Winnie, too, found himself hugging his arch enemy Hercules and gently patting several little mice and cockroaches on the head, and letting his own tears, which were a mixture of happiness and sadness and confusion, flow down his handsome face until they dripped off the end of his long nose.

'I'll only pounce on you and try to catch you,' he said, trying not to choke on his words, 'if you're being *really* naughty and making too much of a mess on the boat... And I really am sorry but I do have to do my job...'

And they all assured him that they understood but that for this one night they were all friends together and would have a wonderful party that none of them would ever forget.

And that's exactly what they did. They danced and they pranced and they sang and they told jokes and they chased each other in pretend-fights in which nobody got hurt and they played party games and promised to do it again next year.

And just as the party was at its height and everybody was feeling on top of the world, the most magical thing of all happened:

All of a sudden they were surrounded on all sides and all the way up to the sky by the ghostly forms of trillions and zillions of moggies and mice and rats and beetles who had died long ago but who had been drawn back by the music and the fun and the camaraderie and who wanted to join in. And, even though Winnie was very scared of ghosts, these ones weren't scary at all, and everybody welcomed them and the party was complete.

And as Winnie sank into his hammock later that night, with Plug humming a soothing sea shanty from his bunk, and all the other little creatures had gone sleepily home, he thought he was the happiest, luckiest moggy in the whole world.

'Good night, dear Plug,' Winnie said. 'I'll never forget this Christmas Eve, never, never, *Never!*'

And he really meant it.

And the memory was still filling his head when, two days later, Plug dropped him off at Number 9 Malekidi Street for his Hols. As usual, the three grown-ups, Loulou, Hissie and Sylvester, were eager to hear all about Winnie's antics at sea (which, of course, he always embroidered to make himself sound bigger and braver and crazier and funnier and cleverer than he really was, but nobody minded because this is what

they all expected anyway and they all loved Winnie so much and his stories made them laugh).

But there was one thing that really did surprise them, something that they could never have expected in a million years:

As they were sitting down to their Christmas lunch (which of course was a couple of days late because they hadn't wanted to celebrate before Winnie came home), Winnie stood up and said he would like to make an announcement. He looked around at the three eager faces and cleared his throat:

'First of all, I want to say Thank You for all these delicious things to eat.' And his eyes scanned everything on the table: the baked sardines, and the mouse and catnip pasties, and the cheesy valerian moussaka, and the big fat lobster which had been a present from Plug and which Hissie and Sylvester had cooked to his special recipe, which contained sea cucumber and toasted Japanese seaweed which had been a present from Mr Tomasaki, a seafaring cat from Okinawa.

'I won't keep you long because I know that you want to tuck into all this lovely food almost as much as I do but I would like to invite Slinky Skinky and his friends to join us at our table...'

From behind his back, Winnie produced a little bowl of crispy fried mosquitoes which he knew were Slinky Skinky's favourite snack, and continued:

'Dear Plug told me all about the snuzzles' Christmas Eve Truce and we had our very own one on the boat and so, even though Slinky Skinky knows that I'm bound to go on chasing him, I want him to know that I wish him no harm, not really, and the same goes for all the other little creatures in the garden and around the house... And let's pretend it's Christmas Eve just for a few hours...'

Seeing the astonished looks on the faces of Loulou and Hissie and Sylvester, Winnie was quick to continue:

'We all know that cats will be cats and that's all there is to it but here and now at Christmas time let's all enjoy ourselves together...'

And he raised his glass of nasturtium champagne (Loulou's speciality) and his voice rang out, 'Happy Christmas, Slinky Skinky! Happy Christmas, *everyone!*'

And as the others lifted their glasses and smiled and wiped away a tear, their voices were raised in Christmas greetings, and Slinky Skinky leapt right

up into Winnie's arms and gave him a friendly lick on the cheek with his long, sticky tongue which made everyone laugh.

You won't be surprised to hear that as soon as the delicious meal was over Winnie was back to his old tricks – swinging by his tail from the lemon tree so that he could reach over the table with his paw and tickle Sylvester's head and pull Loulou's ears and mess up Hissie's fur which she had spent all morning primping and preening so that it looked Just Right.

But nobody minded and they even agreed that it would be all right for him to go down to The Cat's Whiskers later, just as long as he didn't get into trouble and he stayed close to Plug.

What a perfect end to a perfect day!

Or was it? I've got a funny feeling that something is about to go horribly wrong for Winnie...

And sure enough, the young chap was in for a shock:

The trouble was that Winnie had got so used to the idea of Minnie the Mouser and her scary friend The Hoodlum being safely locked away in the Cat Clink Prison that he had completely forgotten that six months had passed and it was time for them to be let out. And, anyway, surely they would have forgotten by now what had happened during their last meeting...

But he was mistaken for not only were the two tough criminals out of prison but they had certainly *not* forgotten the challenge they had made to Winnie all those months ago and which he had been so foolhardy as to accept. In fact, during their long boring months in prison they had talked of very little else, it had been the one thing that had given them pleasure and now they were ready for him!

It was a happy and carefree Winnie who set out that evening, accompanied by Plug (who had had his own Christmas lunch at home with his sister Molly). They both received a huge welcome from all the gang – from Big Mamma and Fat Tom and Toby Toblerone and Gentleman Ginger and the twins Spit and Polish, and all the others. And the laughter was so loud and the catnip beer flowing so generously that nobody, not even dear Plug, noticed the two dark figures slinking in at the back of the crowd. And before he knew it, Winnie felt The Hoodlum's big muddy paw clamped over his mouth and the unmistakable voice of Minnie the Mouser hissing in his ear: 'Don't say a word, else you're a dead mog, got it?!'

Winnie's blood ran cold. Suddenly all those lovely warm Christmassy feelings had vanished and he felt frightened and alone – and he didn't even have his magic co-pilot's cap with him because he hadn't wanted to get it dirty. Oh no...!

'Right!' spat The Hoodlum as soon as they had dragged Winnie behind a pile of old crates where nobody could see them or hear them above the sound of the crashing

music of the Malekidi Monsters. 'Pin back your ears and listen… This is the deal, right? You're gonna spend a night alone in the Castle like wot we all agreed and you've got to do it *soon*, before you go back to your stupid old boat …'

'Yes,' added Minnie in a voice that sounded as cold as steel as she placed her sharp high heel on Winnie's tummy. 'You gotta go through with it this time – no running away like you did before! No running off to tell Auntie Hissie or Auntie Sylvester or Grandad Loulou! You're a big boy now and it's time you started acting like one, got toughened up a bit, right?' And she pressed the sharp point of her heel further into Winnie's tummy so that he yelped, 'Ouch! – yes, all right, I promise, I'll do it, just let me go, I won't say anything to anyone, just let me go, please, you're hurting me, I'll do it, honest…'

'You'd better,' snarled Minnie and The Hoodlum in unison. 'Cos if you don't, you'll be mincemeat – yeah, nice fresh mincemeat! Meet us here tomorrow night at 12 and be sure you come alone…!' And they both laughed a horrible high-pitched bloodcurdling laugh before scampering off into the night, leaving poor Winnie gasping for air and wishing he could wake up and find that it had all been a bad dream.

But it wasn't a dream and so it was a very subdued Winnie who went back into the club to rejoin Plug. He knew he couldn't tell anyone the truth because one thing he knew for sure was that Minnie and her horrible sidekick had been deadly serious. This was something that he, Winnie, would have to face alone.

And as he lay in his basket that night while his dearly beloved Loulou and Hissie and Sylvester slept soundly around him, knowing nothing of his plight, he kept kicking himself and saying under his breath, 'How could I have been so *stupid* in the first place! Why did I want to look like the Big Tough Guy for Minnie! How could I have thought she was pretty and nice?! She's just as horrid and ugly as The Hoodlum!'

And he reached for his treasured co-pilot's cap and touched Hissie's tiny little stitches which held the magic thread in place. And as he did so he seemed to hear a voice from miles away, like tinkling golden bells, which said:

'You can *do* this, Winnie, you *can*! In the last few weeks you've learnt such a lot about love and being strong and holding your head up high, and that's all locked up safely inside you now and nobody can take it away from you. It's going to be scary, yes it is, but you can do it Winnie, yes, you *can*!'

And Winnie eventually fell into a troubled sleep, understanding all too well that tomorrow night would see the start of his biggest, hairiest Adventure yet and it gave him nightmares.

I wouldn't want to be in *his* shoes...

6

WINNIE THE LIONHEART

Winnie woke up with a start. In fact he almost jumped out of his skin. It had been like this all night long – a few minutes of troubled sleep in which he tossed and turned and felt hot and cold, and then a big jolt as he came fully awake and was flooded once again with terror at the thought of what he would have to do tonight.

It was a little after sunrise and, from his basket on the veranda, Winnie could hear Hissie and Sylvester chatting quietly to each other up on the roof as they washed and stretched and got ready for the day. Winnie knew that Loulou was up there too, doing his magical meditation which he always did first thing in the morning.

Knowing they were up there, completely unaware of his troubles, made Winnie feel very sad, and more frightened than ever. All his bounce and swagger had deserted him and his blood ran cold as once again he imagined being locked up all alone in the grim mediaeval castle which had claimed the lives of almost every moggy foolish enough to spend the night within its walls – and, according to the stories he had heard, those few who *had* survived had gone quite mad. Winnie thought he would rather be dead than mad.

Oh dear, oh dear! He was such a *clot*! How could he have been so *stupid*?

But there was no going back now – he knew he had to go through with it. And the worst thing of all was that he couldn't tell anyone, not a single soul – not Plug, not Hissie, not Sylvester, not Loulou. He had never felt so alone and so very small, and his special cosy basket had never felt so dear to him. Would he ever get to spend another night in it, all snuggly and safe?

How was he going to get through the day? And how could he explain the state he was in to the grown-ups? After all, he was shaking like a leaf and he knew that he probably looked as rough as he had done in his bad old days drinking catnip whisky every night down at The Cat's Whiskers.

He put his nose under his paw as if trying to hide from the world. He knew he wouldn't be able to go back to sleep and he was so miserable he almost started to cry. It was a complete nightmare!

And that word – Nightmare – jolted him wide-awake because it had reminded him of something… *Another* nightmare… Yes! He remembered that he had felt just like this when he was still a tiny kitten and had had a dreadful dream. He recalled how Loulou had told him a wonderful story which had made him feel calm and quiet again. If he could just remember that story, perhaps it would work its magic again. What had it been about? Think! he told himself, *Think*! He thought it had had something to do with a brave king who had been facing much worse enemies than Minnie the Mouser and The Hoodlum…

Yes! It was coming back to him now – the brave king had been called Richard, and Winnie could remember how his own frightened kitten-heart had seemed to get bigger and stronger as he listened to Loulou's tale.

Even though he was hazy about the details, Winnie felt a bit better already as if this tiny sliver of memory had freed something inside him and was telling him something important. And then a light bulb flashed on in his brain and he sat bolt upright in his basket. Of course! That was it! This King Richard of Loulou's story had spent time in Limassol Castle! – the very castle where Winnie was going to spend the night!

Immediately he knew what he had to do. He bounded up the lemon tree and on to the roof where Loulou had finished his meditation and was having his early morning wash in the gentle rays of the rising sun.

'Loulou!' Winnie gasped. 'Oh, Loulou, I'm sorry to bother you but I've had the most terrible dreams ALL NIGHT LONG and I feel almost frightened to death. *Please* will you tell me that story again – the one about the snuzzle king, the one you told me when I was very little and had had that scary nightmare? PLEASE!'

Normally Loulou didn't like anything to disturb his morning ritual but one look at Winnie's bloodshot eyes and droopy whiskers told him that his young friend was indeed in a bad way.

'Of course I will,' he said kindly. 'Why don't you curl up here next to my sleeping box. It's a perfect morning for a story.'

And so it was that a few minutes later, with Hissie and Sylvester purring softly beside Winnie, Loulou began:

'Close your eyes and let me take you back more than 800 years,' he said softly. 'It is the year 1191 (the 7th of May) and sailing across the blue Mediterranean Sea is a fleet of ships travelling all the way from England towards Palestine...'

Winnie felt himself start to relax. There was something about Loulou's voice this morning that was dreamy and soothing and Winnie could clearly *see* those magnificent ships with their billowing sails as if he were actually there instead of being curled up with his tail over his nose in the early morning sunshine.

'This fleet of ships,' Loulou went on, 'was under the command of a brave English snuzzle king called Richard. He was very tall and muscly and he didn't know what fear was. Right to the very core of himself he felt strong and sure and this made him very valiant in battle. His men loved him and his enemies respected him and called him "the boldest and most subtle opponent..." *Subtle* means you're cunning and can see exactly what to do when you're in a tight corner... So you see he wasn't only muscly and strong but he was very clever too. And everyone called him King Richard the Lionheart.'

Loulou paused and sat up very tall and straight. 'You'll notice, my friends, that they chose to compare him with a great cat. They could have chosen *any* animal but, no, only that great lion-cat would do. Snuzzles have always recognised and honoured our great strength and intelligence,' he said with pride.

Winnie felt his heart swell. That's what he would be tonight – bold and subtle – and he began to imagine himself just like this 800-year-old King. Maybe everything would be all right, after all.

'At that time,' Loulou continued, 'there were lots of big snuzzle-battles going on right here in and around Cyprus. It seems that snuzzles are *always* fighting about something... These ones, all those years ago, were because both sides thought that their God was the only real one and so they decided they should kill anyone who didn't agree with them...'

Loulou sighed and rolled his eyes and Winnie found himself rolling his own eyes too as he thought of the stupidity of snuzzles, always looking for a fight.

Loulou picked up his story again and as the words rolled off his tongue Winnie had the strangest sensation that the wise old cat was *remembering* this story, as if he were recalling his own past. There was such a ring of Truth in every word and, if Winnie had taken a peek, he would have seen that Loulou had a faraway look in his big green eyes and the corners of his mouth were turned up in a contented smile.

'Well, this brave King Richard the Lionheart was sailing across the sea with lots of soldiers and also Berengaria, the lady he was going to marry, when a great storm blew up and scattered the fleet. Three of the ships were blown right here – close to the old port of Limassol – where they sank and the soldiers either drowned or were taken prisoner by the Governor of Cyprus, a vain and cruel tyrant called Isaac Komnenos.

'And it wasn't only the three ships carrying the soldiers that had been blown close to Limassol in the storm but also the ship carrying Richard's girlfriend, Berengaria.

She was now in great danger. You see, Isaac was very cunning and he sailed out to her ship and pretended to be all nice and friendly, inviting her to come ashore and offering her lots of fresh drinking water for the ship. But what he really planned to do was kidnap her and demand a lot of money from Richard for her release. But Berengaria was also very clever, like her boyfriend, and she guessed that Isaac was lying. So she refused to come ashore and, out of spite, Isaac took back all the drinking water and laughed as her ship went back out into the dark and dangerous waters.

Luckily, the storm settled down soon afterwards and Richard's ship caught up with them. But when he heard about what Isaac had done, he was FURIOUS! – which is something that quite often happens to big brave muscly men, they can have very bad tempers. *Nobody* was going to treat his girlfriend like that! He was ready for a fight!

Winnie's imagination was getting very excited now and he sat up. 'And did all this really happen right here in Limassol?!' he asked breathlessly.

'Yes!' said Loulou. 'Our hometown has been the scene of many great snuzzle battles and dramas for hundreds and hundreds of years... '

Winnie settled back down with his chin on his paws and let his eyes close again so he could more easily picture the scene in his mind's eye. It was just like watching an exciting action movie as Loulou described how, despite his anger, Richard tried to have a meeting with Isaac instead of a battle but Isaac was so rude that Richard got angrier than ever. So, even though many of his men were too sick to fight because of the terrible storm and even though they knew that Isaac had a much bigger army waiting for them on the beach, Richard and a small band of his remaining men sailed towards the shore in small boats called skiffs. They would have to be very clever as well as brave…

'All Isaac's men had rushed down to the shore and thrown loads and loads of things into the water to stop Richard's boats from landing. They had ripped the doors and windows off houses and thrown them into the water, along with huge pieces of wood and broken-down boats and enormous stone jars and all kinds of pots and pans and great big rocks.

'Isaac, who was very vain, was wearing his fanciest clothes and strutting up and down the beach like a silly peacock. And his men were also magnificently dressed in brightly coloured uniforms and with golden banners waving. And they had massive war-horses and big strong mules and they were letting out bloodcurdling screams, like wild dogs howling before a fight.'

Winnie could well imagine what a terrifying sight this must have been for King Richard's men. There they were, just a few of them, rowing towards the shore in their small wooden boats, while an angry crowd of strong, noisy, well-fed men gathered on the beach to confront them.

And, because this part of the story was exciting and even a bit scary, it had taken Winnie's mind completely off Minnie the Mouser and The Hoodlum so he was feeling a lot better. And, as Loulou continued with his tale, it really did sound more and more as if he were describing something he remembered, not just a story from a history book.

He described how, as they approached the shore, King Richard gave a loud command and his archers stood up in their little boats, pulled back their bows and released a huge shower of arrows. And they were such well-trained fighters that it seemed as if there were many more of them than there really were, so that many of Isaac's men panicked and ran away, and some drowned in the waves.

'Despite all the doors and pots and other rubbish which had been thrown into the water to try and stop them, Richard's men managed to pull their skiffs up on to the beach,' Loulou went on. 'And, as soon as they were ashore, not only did the archers continue to shoot great flights of arrows but their comrades threw showers of mighty javelins at the enemy, as well.

'It wasn't easy for King Richard's men,' Loulou said. 'Even though many of Isaac's men had fled, many more stood their ground and fought with great determination for many hours.

'And it was at this point that King Richard showed his true lion's heart for, with fantastic courage, he leapt right out of the boat and into the sea, waving his battleaxe and ready to charge straight on to the beach and fight man-to-man with the enemy. And, as soon as his men saw what their King had done, their own courage returned and their strength increased so that they, too, jumped into the water and marched with their King, still hurling their javelins and releasing arrows and spears as they went.'

Winnie's muscles were twitching now as he imagined himself to be part of that brave band of snuzzles and he honestly felt that he was there in real life as Loulou described how Isaac and the rest of his men turned tail and ran for the safety of the hills.

'By now it was nightfall,' Loulou went on, 'so the king ordered that tents and food should be brought out from the big ships, along with the war-horses which were on board. But many of these poor horses were also very tired and sick because of the terrible storms and so only a few of them were used in the final battle the next day because the men cared about their horses and didn't want them to suffer.

Winnie was happy to hear this. He remembered Loulou telling him a long time ago that you should be kind as well as brave in life and so he was relieved to hear that his new hero, King Richard, was kind to his horses.

He listened intently as Loulou described how, at dawn the next day, King Richard and his remaining 50 men and a few of those horses crept up into the hills to sneak up on Isaac's army. Isaac was still snoring his head off in his tent but a few of his men spotted Richard and his 50 men approaching and they gave a great shout. The final battle was on!

'Isaac's army was far greater than the small crowd around Richard but it was now that Richard's lion's heart could once again truly be seen and it was a sight indeed! The more afraid he knew his men to be, the more courageous he felt himself and that courage flowed into their hearts too.'

Winnie could hardly keep still as Loulou described how Richard finally let his own horse go and charged on foot like a mad bull straight into the first line of enemy soldiers. It was as if he had turned into 10 men, attacking first this group, now that one, waving his sword in one hand and his battleaxe in the other, and bellowing with rage, so that in no time Isaac's soldiers were so freaked out that they started running all over the place in panic and disarray.

'By this time, Isaac had finally pulled on his clothes and rushed out of his tent, only to see his own men fleeing in all directions while the raging King Richard and his small band of soldiers chased after them. Realising he was all alone, Isaac leapt on to his own horse and fled to the mountains, leaving everything – tents and special helmets and breastplates and swords, and gold drinking vessels, and all kinds of rich silk robes, and huge quantities of food and wine – which the victorious English soldiers fell upon with glee (which is what happens after a great battle...)

Loulou stretched and gave a big yawn, as if he himself had indeed been fighting strenuously all night. He looked at Winnie and smiled:

'Are you feeling any better now, young man?' he asked. 'Just imagine! All that excitement – all that noise and all those horses and soldiers charging about, right here on our doorstep! Snuzzles certainly do like a drama!'

'But wait a minute, Loulou!' Hissie and Sylvester said in unison, before Winnie had been able to answer Loulou's question, 'What about King Richard's girlfriend, Berengaria? That isn't the end of the story! What about *her*?!'

Loulou smiled and said, 'You're quite right, ladies, I forgot to end the story properly... I was thinking of young Winnie here and how he would probably prefer a story of heroics rather than romance!'

Winnie nodded his head up and down with great vigour. He had no time for romance! He had felt romantic about Minnie the Mouser and look where *that* had got him!

'But the ladies are quite right,' Loulou added. 'I'll tell them the whole story later but just for now let me say that, after his great victory, Richard brought Berengaria ashore and, together with all their men and companions, they travelled to Limassol Castle where they had tremendous celebrations and Richard and Berengaria were married and she became his Queen.'

At this, Hissie got a gooey look on her face and so did Sylvester because, even though she was often more of a tomboy than an elderly lady-cat, she was also still a girl at heart. They both sighed with contentment. It was all very well for Winnie to have an exciting tale of derring-do but that wasn't enough for the ladies, they wanted a happy ending all round.

It had taken Loulou an hour to tell his tale because he had spoken very slowly in that mesmerising voice of his and had sometimes acted out snippets of the more dramatic moments, such as the archers showering their arrows and the king leaping into the sea with the courage of a lion.

And as Loulou's tale came to its close, Winnie felt much better. He *would* be all right tonight, he told himself. He was going to stay the night in the very castle where brave King Richard had celebrated his victory and had married his Queen. Surely something of the King's courageous spirit would still be there, in the castle, to help him in his hour of need! He would imagine he *was* Richard the Lionheart and he *would* survive this night all alone in that dreadful place! He would *not* die or go mad like those other moggies he had heard about...! And with that comforting thought, he at last fell into a peaceful sleep.

There was still a long day to get through before his midnight meeting with Minnie the Mouser and The Hoodlum but Winnie had only been asleep for two hours (which is a very short sleep for a cat) when he was awoken by a tremendous commotion coming from Katie Snuzzle's living room. In two seconds flat he was wide awake again, and so were all the grown-ups. What was going on? They could hear loud snuzzle voices and the next thing was that Katie was coming out into the garden with her arm around the shoulder of her friend Valerie, who was in floods of tears.

At first, Winnie couldn't make out what they were saying, it was just a great big muddle of sobs and indistinct words. What *was* clear, however, was that something catastrophic had happened. Loulou, Hissie and Sylvester had also heard the racket and were peering over the edge of the flat roof, straining their ears to try and understand what was going on.

The two friends were now sitting on wicker chairs and Katie was giving her friend a glass of cool home-made lemonade to calm her nerves.

'When did you last see her?' Katie asked gently. 'When did this terrible thing happen?'

'Last night,' Valerie replied. 'It was such a warm evening that she settled down to sleep on the balcony, instead of coming inside with me. I didn't notice she was gone until this morning. I've hunted high and low and I even went downstairs all around the block of flats just in case she had jumped off the balcony... Oh, I can't bear to think about it...' And she started sobbing all over again.

'Where, can she *be*?' she wailed. 'She couldn't possibly survive all on her own out in the big wide world. She's got those wonky back legs and only one eye. She wouldn't stand a chance with all those scary wild moggies out there. And I don't know where to *begin* looking for her...'

Trying to be as invisible as possible, Winnie got out of his basket, tiptoed to the bottom of the lemon tree and then climbed up it as quietly as possible so he could join the grown-ups on the roof.

'What's it all about, Loulou?' Winnie whispered. 'Who is she talking about?'

'It must be Chloe Cuddlebucket. She's the middle-aged lady-cat who lives with Valerie Snuzzle. I've often overheard Valerie and our own Katie talking about Miss Chloe. She moved in with Valerie a few years ago, having had a very difficult start in life – a drunken snuzzle ran over her in his car when she was very small. That's why she's got those wonky legs and only one eye that Valerie mentioned a minute ago.'

Loulou paused for a moment and his forehead was knitted into a puzzled frown. 'I know that they live on the fourth floor of a block of flats so Chloe doesn't normally go out at all, other than on to the balcony. I know that we all like to have the freedom to wander about all over the place – especially you, young Winnie – but, with her difficulties, Chloe's happy to stay in her own little world up in their fourth-floor flat.

So *why* would she suddenly decide to leave? And *how* could she leave anyway? She can't fly and she hasn't got a magic carpet like we have... What a mystery! No wonder Valerie is in such a state.'

'Oh I wish there was something we could *do*!' Hissie and Sylvester said at the same time. 'Any ideas, Loulou?'

But Loulou shook his head. 'I wouldn't know where to begin,' he said. 'I'm as much in the dark as the snuzzles are.' He frowned again. 'But I'm definitely going to make some enquiries,' he said. 'You know how hopeless snuzzles can be when there's a crisis. They completely lose their heads and can't think straight. They're going to need a lot of help from us so we all need to get our thinking caps on.'

'Richard the Lionheart would know what to do!' Winnie said enthusiastically. '*He* would find her!'

By this time, Katie had persuaded her friend to go for a walk with her to clear her head and calm her down. 'And then we'll have lunch at a nice cafe and I'll take you home,' she said. 'I'm sure everything will work out all right and you will have Chloe home again in no time.'

(To be honest, Katie wasn't nearly as confident as she sounded but she knew she had to say things that would make her friend strong enough to face whatever happened. That's what true friends do, they say just the right thing at the right time.)

There were still several hours before Winnie was due to meet up with Minnie the Mouser and The Hoodlum at The Cat's Whiskers. He had managed to arrange it so that Plug would take him there at nine o'clock so all he had to figure out was how to sneak away from Plug's protective gaze in time to be behind the crates at midnight for his dangerous assignation with the two crooks.

He spent the rest of the day trying as hard as possible to relax. He tried to use some advice he had been given by Mog Dahl (that mysterious old Indian cat who had disappeared at the top of the coil of rope) and tried to breathe in through one nostril and out through the other so that first his left whiskers and then his right whiskers rustled gently like a breeze in the trees. But he couldn't concentrate. Instead he found it better to keep imagining he was Richard the Lionheart and that he would be able to feel that brave King's strong muscles and great courage rippling through him when he was inside spooky old Limassol Castle in just a few hours' time.

'What's up, old chap?' Plug asked as they were walking towards The Cat's Whiskers that evening 'You're all of a jitter...'

'I'm all right, thanks,' Winnie mumbled, staring at his own feet as they meandered along. 'Just a bit tired, that's all.'

'I understand,' Plug said kindly. 'Tell you what – I know you won't get into any scrapes so how about, when we get to the Club, I go off and have a game of dominoes with Bob and Bert so you don't feel I'm breathing down your neck? I'll come looking for you when it's time to go home, OK?'

'Thanks mate,' said Winnie, 'that would be really great...' He was trying to sound cheerful but he was in two minds. It's true that Plug's suggestion meant he would be able to sneak off much more easily when the time came but part of him would much rather have known that Plug was, indeed, keeping a strict eye on him.

Once they were inside The Cat's Whiskers, Plug bought them each a bottle of catnip beer and went off to find his friends. Winnie took his drink to a quiet table in the corner and tried to look inconspicuous. He was in no mood for dancing or small talk, he just wanted midnight to come as soon as possible so the whole thing would be over.

He clutched his little knapsack to his chest, comforting himself with the knowledge that it contained his magical co-pilot's cap, along with some mouse and mint sandwiches he'd stolen from Hissie's secret larder behind the water butt. He was sure she would forgive him if she knew the fix he was in.

The place wasn't very crowded at this time of the evening, just a few couples at other tables and a group of three surly-looking ginger toms skulking at one end of the bar. It was clear they had already drunk a lot of catnip whisky, and the drunker they got the louder they spoke so that Winnie was able to listen in to their conversation without being observed.

'That was a good night's work!' the biggest of the three tomcats said in a loud rasping whisper. 'That ransom's going to set me up for life! *Very* nice!' he added, rubbing his grubby paws together.

'Shhh!' the other two said in unison. 'There won't be any ransom if you go shouting about it, Jezza! Keep your blinking voice down!'

Winnie's ears pricked up. A ransom! That was money that criminals demanded when they'd kidnapped someone! This was a criminal gang! And they looked even meaner and rougher than The

Hoodlum... Winnie craned his neck as far as he could in their direction without being seen, and strained all the nerves in his ears to try and pick up their conversation, which was now being conducted at a lower volume.

'Princess Primrose,' the one called Jezza was saying. 'A pretty name for my passport to prosperity! That super-wealthy Russian geezer won't have any trouble coming up with the money and I know he dotes on that pampered pedigree puss so he's bound to meet our demands!' And he rubbed his paws together again.

'But what if he doesn't?' asked one of his sidekicks. 'Maybe he doesn't care about her as much as you think...'

'Of course he does,' Jezza sneered. Then he took another swig of his whisky, wiped his mouth with the back of his paw and said, 'But if he *doesn't* turn up with the readies by 5am like what I put in the ransom note, then we'll just have to get rid of her...'

'What do you mean by that?' the other conspirators muttered.

'That's obvious!' said Jezza. 'You weren't born yesterday, were you? We'll have to...' and he made a horrible cutting motion across his throat with his paw.

The others gasped. 'You don't mean *kill* her, do you, Boss?'

'Course I do! Don't tell me you've gone soft! If we don't get a ransom this time we'll just kidnap some other pampered madam until we do. Anyway, it won't come to that. I made it quite clear in my note we'd hand her over at five o'clock in the morning. All he's got to do is bring the money in a brown paper bag and, in the meantime, we can get nicely sozzled here, knowing that Princess Primrose is safely tucked away where no one will find her.'

And he gave a loud burp.

Well, well, Winnie said to himself. *Another* innocent moggy in trouble! I wouldn't want to be at the mercy of that lot! Minnie the Mouser and The Hoodlum look like chickenfeed compared to that bunch! And he ordered himself another catnip beer and went outside for a gentle little dance under the trees. Maybe it wouldn't be so bad after all...

All this time, Plug had been enjoying several games of mouse dominoes with his pals. In fact he was feeling very chirpy as he had won several free drinks during the course of the evening.

'I'm one lucky moggy!' he chuckled to himself as he looked at his watch and, seeing that it was five minutes to midnight, decided it was time he went in search of Winnie. But, as Plug was about to find out, he wasn't going to feel like a lucky moggy for long...

Winnie had already set off in the direction of the crates for his rendezvous with Minnie and The Hoodlum. However much he had been dreading the whole thing, he certainly didn't want to be late. Seeing that Plug was still engrossed in his game with his chums, Winnie had given him the slip in plenty of time. He felt bad about it – he had never deceived Plug before – and part of him still wished he could think of some way out. But no, the terrible moment had arrived.

Just as he approached the pile of crates he heard a horrible 'thwacking' sound behind him and spun round, half expecting to find The Hoodlum creeping up on him. But to his horror he saw that Minnie and her partner in crime had actually been creeping up on Plug.

Oh no! Winnie thought to himself. Plug must have been coming out to find me and the Dreadful Duo have coshed him!

Sure enough, Plug was lying on the ground, out cold, and Minnie and The Hoodlum were slapping each other on the back and giggling.

'That'll teach him!' The Hoodlum snarled. 'The last thing we need is that old codger sticking his nose in!' And they both laughed again.

Winnie was furious. How dare they call his dear friend Plug 'an old codger'! And he was delighted to discover that his anger made him feel stronger – just like King Richard the Lionheart felt stronger when he was angry and his blood was up.

'I'll show 'em,' Winnie muttered under his breath. 'I'll give them something to think about!'

But before he knew what was happening Minnie had grabbed his back legs in a rugby tackle and The Hoodlum had kicked him in the tummy and pulled a rough sack over his head so he couldn't see anything.

'Not a peep out of you!' they both hissed. 'If you let out the tiniest miaow, you won't be as lucky as your stupid old friend back there... Got it? You'll get such a clobber on the back of the head you'll never wake up again!'

Winnie scarcely dared breathe as he found himself being dragged along by the scruff of his neck. The two crooks were running fast, not wanting to be spotted by any moggies or snuzzles who might still be out and about at this time of night, and they didn't care that Winnie was being battered and bruised as they pulled him along over the rough ground.

And, even though Winnie had been dreading the thought of arriving at the castle, the journey there was so painful that he suddenly wanted to get there very quickly indeed.

At last his tormentors came to a halt and, although Winnie could hear them scrabbling around in the dark, he couldn't see a thing. There was a lot of scraping and whispering and the sound of a big stone being dragged slowly to one side and then, with an almighty shove on his bum, he was pushed through a narrow gap and into a cold, dark space. Minnie's paw shot through and yanked the rough sack off his head at the same time as The Hoodlum hissed, 'You're done for, mate! By this time tomorrow you'll either be dead or mad! Toodle-oo!' And then Winnie heard the big stone sliding back into place and, as if from a great distance, he could just hear the two crooks laughing their heads off as they scampered away into the night.

It took Winnie a couple of minutes to get his breath back and begin to assess the situation. He rubbed his paws over his bruises and all of a sudden began to feel tearful and wished – oh, *how* he wished – that Sylvester and Hissie would appear to give him one of their lovely rub-downs. But no, he told himself severely, no tears for Winnie! I want to stay angry – very, very angry! That way I'll stay alive and I won't go mad.

Gradually his magical night-vision got stronger and he was able to see where he was. He was in a large stone chamber which seemed to be almost empty except for the spooky shadows which shivered and shuddered all around him. He could hear scurryings coming from the far end and when he narrowed his eyes to slits so as to see better, he could make out some rat-holes and he caught the glimpse of a disappearing tail and the glint of a malevolent red eye. Gosh! That rat was even bigger than Hercules! Winnie took a deep breath and gulped.

There didn't seem to be anywhere to hide and he didn't fancy the idea of the huge rat coming back with all his friends. Although Winnie had caught loads of rats on board ship, his imagination was running away with him now and he envisaged himself being hunted down by an army of the giant rodents. Maybe that's how all the other moggies had died... Oh dear, it was just like a horror film! But No, he reminded himself again even more severely, it was just those kind of thoughts that would make him go mad. He *must* stay strong.

Two minutes later, by which time his eyes had got used to the darkness, he had the fright of his life! He noticed a tall and extremely creepy shape against the wall opposite him. It looked like a snuzzle except that it was absolutely *massive*. It had big feet and arms and legs and a strange helmet on its head and it stood very tall and straight and still as if it were ready to jump out at him. What on earth...?

But of course! Loulou had told him how the snuzzle soldiers used to cover themselves in heavy metal armour to protect them in battle. This must be a suit of armour! Maybe it was *King Richard's* suit of armour! Wow!

Winnie was about to creep across the stone floor to check if he was right when he was startled by another lot of scurrying behind him which made him stop in his tracks and look over his shoulder, scarcely able to breathe. What was coming after him? Maybe he was completely surrounded by an army of super-rats! And then, as if he weren't scared enough already, a high-pitched wailing sound began to come from *inside* the suit of armour. Oh Lord! Don't tell me it's alive, Winnie gasped. Maybe there's the ghost of an old snuzzle-soldier in there! Oh no, oh no, oh no...!

But then everything went quiet again – *completely silent* – and Winnie began creeping very slowly and gingerly in the general direction of the suit of armour. His plan was to hide behind it. After all, he told himself, there was nowhere else for him to hide, even if the armour *was* haunted by a scary ghost.

As he got closer, he began to make out the details of the armour itself. It certainly was very big and must have been tremendously heavy to wear in battle. Snuzzles certainly were very peculiar creatures. Just imagine them all clanking about on the battlefield! The idea almost made him laugh even though he was so terrified.

But just then he heard the high-pitched wailing sound again and, yes, it *was* coming from inside the suit of armour. Maybe it would attack him... Maybe it would snatch him up in its big metal fingers and throttle him... Maybe this was all part of Minnie and The Hoodlum's evil plan!

The sound was getting louder now and even more high-pitched so Winnie was able to hear what it was saying for, yes, it was a *voice*:

'Help! Help me!' the voice pleaded. *'Please* help me!'

Winnie froze. The armour wasn't going to attack him at all. It was a very different story. Somebody was trapped inside it and by the sound of it they were even more scared than he was...

'Who are you?' Winnie whispered. But then, realising that a whisper wouldn't be heard through the thick metal, he repeated loudly, 'Who are you, who *are* you?!'

'My name is Chloe,' came the reply. Chloe Cuddlebucket... And who are *you*? Have you come to help me or hurt me?' The voice was trembling.

Winnie was in a whirl of confusion. Where had he heard that name before? It seemed very familiar but in all the excitement of the past few hours his mind was playing tricks on him and he couldn't remember anything.

'My name's Winnie,' he called back. 'I won't hurt you, I promise. I've been thrown in here myself and I really want to get out but I don't know how. How did you get inside there?'

'The only thing I remember is that a horrid big tomcat put something with a terrible smell over my nose and the next thing was that I woke up and found myself trapped in here, all alone, and with a pounding headache. Oh, *please* can you get me out of here?' She sounded desperate.

'I can't see *how* to get you out! It looks like the only opening is in the helmet – where the snuzzle's face would have been – but I can't reach it...' He thought for a moment and then shouted excitedly, 'Ooh, I've got an idea! It'll be very uncomfortable for you and it'll shake you all about but I'm going to make the armour topple over so it's down on the ground and then I'll be able to let you out. OK?'

'Yes!' shouted the poor trapped moggy from deep inside. 'I don't mind how scary or noisy it is, just get me out! I've been in here for ages and ages and I'd do *anything* to get out!'

'All right then!' Winnie shouted back. And he gathered all his strength and leapt a huge mighty leap – a leap worthy of a courageous king – until he was right on top of the helmet of the suit of armour and hanging on with all his strength. It was very difficult because he couldn't dig his claws into the metal and he kept almost sliding off. But, with a huge effort, he managed to wrap his paws all the way around the neck part of the armour and then he began bouncing backwards and forwards and backwards and forwards until, *wallop*, the whole thing started to topple over.

There was the most almighty crash as the armour hit the stone floor and Winnie leapt from his perch just in time.

'You all right, Miss Chloe?!' he called out anxiously. 'That was a heck of a crash!'

'Yes, thank you,' came the rather shaky reply from inside. 'I had a bit of a bump on my behind but other than that I think I'm fine.'

'All right,' Winnie called. 'I'm going to prise the helmet open now and you'll be able to squeeze out if you pull your tummy in.'

And in ten seconds flat the helmet was open and Winnie was helping a very shaken but very thankful middle-aged lady-cat out into the chamber, whereupon she burst into great sobs and hurled herself into his arms.

'My hero!' she sobbed. 'You've saved my life! Thank you, oh, *thank you!*'

And, forgetting his own fear for a moment, Winnie felt his heart swell with pride. He *was* a hero! – a real proper hero! Wow! And even though it was dark and not really the right time to care about his image, Winnie scrabbled about in his little backpack with the one hand that wasn't holding on to Chloe and dug out his co-pilot's cap. He pulled it on at what he guessed to be a jaunty angle and thought, Now I *look* more like a hero, which is just what I need to be tonight.

He took a deep breath and returned his attention to his sobbing companion:

'So, madam,' he said, trying to sound as brave and grown-up as possible, 'What happened to you? What's your story?'

Dabbing at her eye with her paw, Chloe said, 'I'll explain in a moment but don't you think you should tell me who *you* are first?'

'Of course,' said Winnie quickly, 'my name is Winnie and I live with Loulou, Hissie and Sylvester at Number 9 Malekidi Street here in Limassol. And we have a snuzzle called Katie.'

'Katie Snuzzle?!' Chloe exclaimed. 'But Katie is my own snuzzle's friend. *Her* name is Valerie. Do you know her?'

'Yes, I most certainly do!' Winnie said excitedly. 'I've known her since I was a kitten and she often comes for tea with Katie. In fact, she was there this morning, crying her eyes out because...'

He suddenly shut up. Of course! That's where he had heard the name Chloe Cuddlebucket before! This unfortunate lady-cat locked up with him in Limassol Castle was Valerie's missing moggy!

'But what *happened* Miss Chloe? I mean, why are you here in the castle?' Winnie's words came tumbling out all in a rush. 'I truly don't know,' Chloe said. 'I'd been snoozing out on the balcony for a couple of hours and I was still there when Valerie went to bed. That often happens and then when it starts getting chilly outside I creep inside and join her. But last night, last night...' Her voice trailed off again. 'Oh, I can't *remember*...'

'Please *try!*' Winnie urged. 'Surely you can remember *something?*'

Chloe's voice had gone very quiet as she tried to concentrate.

'It's no good,' she murmured, 'it's all a blur.'

Winnie sighed but then had one of his brainwaves. He scrabbled about in the dark for his backpack and pulled something out:

'Here!' he said. 'You must be starving! I knew I was going to have a long night so I brought some mouse and mint sandwiches with me. They're a bit squashed but they'll make you feel better.' And the next moment Chloe was munching hungrily and beginning to feel her strength come back.

'You're quite right, Winnie! I haven't eaten for over 24 hours and I'm ravenous! These really are delicious!' And she chomped her way through two more of Winnie's sandwiches. And as she did so, there flashed into her mind an image of two ruffians and a bright light and then a horrible sweet smell that made her feel sick and then everything had gone black.

As she explained this to Winnie, he tried to put two and two together.

'Do you think you've been kidnapped?' he asked. 'Is that possible?'

'But I'm on the fourth floor of a block of flats near the sea. Valerie is very careful to lock up the front door at night and the only other way to get in would be to climb all the way up on the outside and that's a sheer drop. Surely nobody could climb up that way? '

'But you must have heard of cat-burglars!' Winnie said. 'They *can* run up the sides of buildings! They hang on by their long claws which have metal tips to make them extra strong...'

'But who would want to kidnap *me*?' Chloe wailed. 'I've only got one eye and rather wonky back legs. I'm not exactly a prize specimen! I'm not a pedigree. I'm not worth loads and loads of money...'

'I'm sure you are worth loads and loads of money to Valerie,' Winnie said. 'But I do agree, it's very strange. You see, just this evening I heard about *another* moggy who's been kidnapped. She's called Princess Primrose and she lives with a wealthy Russian gentleman and she *is* worth a lot of money and they demanded a ransom for her.' He shuddered as he remembered what that big bruiser Jezza had threatened to do to her if the gent didn't pay up.

'Princess Primrose!' Chloe exclaimed. 'But I know her! She lives in the penthouse flat just above me and we quite often have conversations when we are both out on our balconies. She's very nice, even though she's so posh, and it is true, her Russian gentleman loves her as much as Valerie loves me and he has masses and masses of money and *would* pay a lot of it to have her back. It's all a mystery...'

But it was starting to be less of a mystery to Winnie and he felt his blood run cold. It was obvious what had happened. Those two blundering idiots who worked for Jezza had snatched the wrong moggy! Valerie Snuzzle hadn't received a ransom note – she would have mentioned it to Katie if she had – and even if Princess Primrose's Russian gentleman *had* received a ransom note, he would simply have laughed and thrown it away. After all, his Princess Primrose was still safe and sound at home, he would have thought the whole thing was a joke – not a very nice joke, but a joke all the same.

So that meant...

Oh dear, he scarcely dared think about it...

No ransom would be paid at the time Jezza and his partners in crime expected and... Once again he remembered that horrible throat-cutting action of Jezza's. At five o'clock, they would be here to carry out their dreadful threat! He must think of something! He must *do* something! He couldn't let this nice lady-cat, who was very like his own beloved Aunties, Hissie and Sylvester, come to such a sticky end. And, above all, he mustn't let Chloe *know* that she had been taken by mistake. It was clear to Winnie that she was completely confused and hadn't yet understood what had happened. If she thought she only had a few more hours to live she might get hysterical (Winnie had heard somewhere that this occasionally happened to middle-aged lady-cats) and then it would be even more difficult to think up a plan.

He must think, think, *think*...!

'Don't worry, Miss Chloe,' he said, touching his peaked cap and reminding himself that, if he ever found himself in truly mortal danger, he could touch that magic golden thread and summon Loulou and the magic carpet. But he also remembered how Loulou had impressed upon him that there was no 100% guarantee and also that he had to wait till *the very last moment* before touching it, otherwise it wouldn't work.

'Just you try to relax,' he said, stiffening his spine and trying to sound heroic. 'I'm sure there's a perfectly reasonable explanation for this whole mess and our two very clever snuzzles will find us in no time. We've still got a few mouse and mint sandwiches to share and I could tell you a story that you might like – a story about this very castle.'

And, with his mind still racing and trying to figure out a means of escape, he began to tell her all about brave King Richard the Lionheart and the way he had rescued his girlfriend Berengaria and married her right here in Limassol Castle. He remembered how much he had enjoyed all the details about the battles that Loulou had described but he also remembered that Hissie and Sylvester had both wanted to hear about the romantic side of the story – that's what ladies liked.

So, instead of saying too much about the battles which he thought might unsettle Chloe even more, he spent more time describing how handsome King Richard was and how magnificent he looked astride his horse or standing at the front of the boat shouting commands to his men. And he told her that his girlfriend Berengaria was the most beautiful snuzzle who had ever lived, even though he had no idea whether this was true or not. All that mattered was that he helped this poor kidnapped moggy to relax. And, even though Winnie did not know it, it was just this sort of kindness when he was in danger himself which marked him out as a real hero. Real heroes always have some courage and good-heartedness left over to help other people – or other moggies.

And it did the trick. By the time Winnie had got to the bit where he was describing the romantic wedding that had taken place right here in the castle between King Richard and his new Queen, Miss Chloe had a dreamy look on her face and she even began to purr quietly to herself and eventually fell into a doze.

Only when he was sure that she was asleep did Winnie stop telling his tale and allow himself a few moments of rest. In the short time that he had known this unusual little lady with her wonky back legs and one bright green eye, he had become very fond of her and felt protective towards her in an extremely grown-up sort of way. Perhaps, he thought, some of King Richard's chivalry and magic really was creeping into his own frightened body and heart. And he saw that Miss Chloe was a bit like Berengaria really – through no fault of her own, she was at the mercy of ruthless crooks and her life was in danger. Only he, Winnie the Lionheart, stood between her and a horrible death. This thought made him feel more frightened than ever but in a strange way it also made him feel stronger than he could have imagined. Danger is a very peculiar thing...

It was so dark in the chamber that Winnie couldn't tell what time it was. The minutes were ticking by – and all the mouse and mint sandwiches had gone – but whether one hour or three hours had passed he couldn't be sure. All he knew was

that somehow he had to come up with a brilliant idea before five o'clock when the ruffians would be back to break in and carry out their terrible threat.

He drifted in and out of a light and fitful sleep, waking every few minutes with a jump and then dozing off again, only to wake again a few minutes later. To his relief, each time he checked on Chloe he found that she was slumbering peacefully.

From time to time he heard the scurryings of the rats at the far end of the chamber and leapt to his feet, ready to do battle. But they weren't interested in him but kept to themselves, occasionally squabbling over a piece of food.

But what was *that*?! This sound was different. It was a loud scraping sound and Winnie was instantly wide-awake. This time there was no doubting it. He recognised that sound only too well. It was the noise of the big stone being dragged aside, the stone which covered the entrance hole through which the crooks had pushed him and Chloe a few hours earlier. It must be five o'clock!

This time the noise had also woken Chloe. She recognised it too and, even though she didn't know as much as Winnie did about the danger they were both in, she did know that things were looking bad. Her heart was hammering in her chest and she crept closer to Winnie for protection.

He put his arm around her shoulder and coaxed her gently round behind the fallen suit of armour which was stretched out on the floor and at the same time he put all his attention and all his effort into imagining that King Richard's bravery and huge muscles were pouring into his own trembling body.

He tried to figure out what would be the best way of attacking the two – or maybe even three – kidnappers when they finally got the stone open enough to let them into the chamber. But his mind was in a whirl and he couldn't think straight. Calm down! he told himself sternly. Think, boy, *think*! Should he spring at them as they came in – take them by surprise? Or should he just sneak silently around the edge of the chamber and try to escape from behind their backs? But what about Miss Chloe? *He* might be able to move swiftly enough to get past them but he knew that Chloe's back legs weren't strong enough and he couldn't possibly carry her and get them both through the gap in a matter of seconds.

The scraping sound got louder and louder and now they could also hear the rough voices of Jezza's gang. It was clear they were tanked up with catnip whisky and were squabbling amongst themselves. This was looking worse and worse, Winnie thought. He knew there was no way he would be able to talk to them and explain that there had been a terrible mistake and that this lady-cat was not Princess Primrose at all. If he told them that, particularly in their drunken state, it would be likely to make them more furious than ever and they would probably take it out on Chloe and himself with even more cruelty.

The armour was standing completely upright and it was walking!

By now the stone had been pulled aside sufficiently for a glimmer of early morning light to have fallen through the entrance and Winnie could see the first of the ruffians shouldering his way into the chamber. The grating sound intensified as his two companions continued to heave the stone the last few inches and, in her terror, Miss Chloe broke away from the safety of Winnie's embrace and leapt wildly on to the back of the fallen armour.

And as she did so, the most extraordinary thing happened: with a huge shudder and an almighty clanking sound, the suit of armour began to get to its feet and Chloe slid right off and on to the stone-flagged floor. Winnie couldn't believe his eyes. The light coming from the entrance was now bright enough for him to see that the armour was standing completely upright and – oh, my goodness! – it was *walking*!

Not only that, but the entire scene was changing before his very eyes!

The walls were evaporating, the castle disappearing, and now there was open ground beneath his paws – open ground which was being churned up by men's feet and horses' hooves. The air was thick with the sound of clashing and crashing, of snuzzle soldiers shouting at each other, and a high-pitched whine as hails of arrows flew overhead.

Chloe was right beside him and Winnie grabbed her paw just in time to stop her from being crushed under the heavy feet of a soldier in full armour who was waving his battleaxe like a madman.

'Wh...what's happening...?' Chloe whimpered. 'Is this a dream, Winnie? Am I awake?'

'No, it's not a dream!' Winnie bellowed above the deafening noise of the battle which was raging all around them. 'Somehow we've gone zooming back in time... We must keep out of harm's way as best we can!'

And he half dragged her, zigzagging this way and that, until they were crouching behind a small tree.

'We'll be safe here for a minute or two,' Winnie said, his mind racing. 'Keep your head down and I'll stay on watch and plan what to do...'

It had all happened so fast! One minute they had been in the spooky dark castle and the next, here they were, in broad daylight, in the midst of a wild snuzzle battle. Chloe shut her one eye tight and clamped her paws firmly over her ears, telling herself that if she couldn't see or hear what was going on nothing could hurt her.

But Winnie was surprised to discover that he was more excited than afraid. He was a knight in shining armour with a Fair Lady to protect! He was Winnie the Lionheart! At that very moment a stray arrow whizzed through the air just above their heads and Winnie shot up his paw and caught it, just like that! Wow! he thought, I'm a genius, I'm amazing...!

Chloe, who was still trying to shut out all the noises and scary sights about her, hadn't seen this clever stunt, which was probably just as well. But Winnie was cock-a-hoop with the thrill of it all and he tapped on Chloe's shoulder and shouted, 'Come on! I can see some big rocks and sand dunes over there so, if we run very quickly, we'll be able to find ourselves a better hiding place and we can watch the action without being in danger. OK?'

And before she had time to answer, Chloe was being pulled along by Winnie at great speed so that the terrifying sounds died down a little and then they both dived into a clump of tussocky grass on the top of a dune and lay there for a few moments catching their breath.

'Wheee!' said Winnie. 'We're a bit higher up here so we'll be able to look down and see exactly what's going on.'

They lay side-by-side on their tummies, their ears pricked up, their eyes sharp, and their chins pressing into the sand so as to keep their heads down and out of sight.

'Don't you think it's time to touch that magic thread in your cap, the one you told me about before?' Chloe asked. 'Surely we've been in enough danger for Loulou and that magic carpet to come and rescue us...'

'I can't do that just yet,' Winnie explained. 'While we're here behind this sand dune, we're *not* really in mortal danger and if I touch the thread when it's not absolutely necessary, it won't help and then it might not work when we really *do* need it. I'm sorry but we're going to have to wait a bit longer.'

'It might not *seem* as if we are in danger,' Chloe went on, 'but when Loulou gave you that special cap with its magic golden thread he didn't say anything about time travelling, did he?'

'That's true,' Winnie agreed. 'But Something deep inside me tells me that I'll know the exact moment when I need to touch it so we can have the best chance of being rescued. I almost touched it back there in the castle but that same Something pulled my paw back at the last moment and it happened again just before we ran off behind the tree. I can't explain it but, even though it felt as if something terrible was about to happen, I *knew* that I mustn't touch it quite yet...'

They lay there in silence for a minute and then Winnie said: 'Isn't it strange to think that it will be another 800 years before Loulou or Hissie or Sylvester or you or I or our dear snuzzles are even born! Right now there is no Number 9 Malekidi Street – in fact, there isn't even a Malekidi Street, let alone a Number 9!'

'Well we can't stay here forever!' Chloe pointed out. 'Do you think we can change history?'

'Of course we can!' said Winnie. 'Cats can do anything!

'I mean,' Chloe went on, 'we both know we've had hundreds and thousands of lives already and we'll have hundreds and thousands more in the future but...' (and here her voice went rather quiet and sad) '...the thing is I was enjoying the life I was having right now – or do I mean right *then*? And I hate to think I might never get it back again... Oh Winnie, you do think we'll get home all right, don't you?'

'I'm sure we will,' Winnie said giving her shoulder a squeeze. 'We are playing an important part in history and we've got Magic on our side. After all, how on earth could I have caught this if I hadn't got Magic on my side?' And he showed her the arrow he had caught when her eye had been tight shut. 'And I'm sure it was an arrow belonging to King Richard's side, not to that scoundrel Isaac.'

'How long should we stay here?' Chloe asked. 'What do you think we should do to *help* King Richard and his men?'

'I'm not sure,' Winnie said thoughtfully, as if this was something he had been pondering carefully for a long time. 'But what I do know is that we must get ourselves some food if we are going to be energetic and useful moggies.'

'That shouldn't be difficult,' Chloe said. 'After all, we're very close to the sea so there must be some fish around here somewhere – perhaps some little ones in those rock pools over there... I'm sure you could easily catch a fish, Winnie, you're so clever!'

'You're quite right!' Winnie said. 'That's one of the things Plug and I often do on our afternoons off when we're at sea. I'm very quick at grabbing little shrimps out of the water and straight into my mouth. I'll run over there and bring us some back – but the only thing I've got to put them in is my cap so I hope Loulou won't be cross with me if it's in a bit of a state when I eventually see him again.'

Chloe smiled for the first time in many many hours. 'I'm sure the last thing he will think about is being cross with you,' she said. 'And the truth is, Winnie, it's already pretty bashed-up after everything it's been through in the last few hours. All that *really* matters is that the magic thread stays safely in place.'

'I'm sure it will,' Winnie said confidently. 'Hissie is *very* careful with everything she does – cooking, sewing, massaging my back when I've been showing off too much...'

'Well then, we haven't really got anything to worry about, have we?' Chloe said, trying to sound brave.

'I won't be long!' Winnie said as he bounded off in the direction of the rock pools a hundred yards away. 'Just remember to keep your head down but also see if you can keep your eye on the battlefield in case there are any major developments that we need to know about.'

Winnie was as good as his word.
His skill as a shrimp fisherman had
never been more important to him
than it was now and in fifteen
minutes his cap was crammed
full of a delicious dinner which
included, not only shrimps, but
several small fish and two hermit
crabs as well. He had even gathered a
little bit of bright green seaweed because

Hissie had always told him to put some salad on
his plate because it was good for him and would also make the food *look* more delicious
which was very important. The first time she had told him this, he thought it sounded
silly but later on, when he noticed that Plug always followed this same rule when he was
preparing a meal at sea, he had decided it must be a good idea after all.

He had just set off to run the hundred yards back towards the sand dune when he
heard a terrified shriek. It was Chloe's voice! What now?! He ran as fast as he could
and the screaming got louder and louder and then he saw why. An enormous dog was
racing towards Chloe, baying like a wolf, its fangs glistening.

Winnie hurtled onwards as fast as his legs could carry him. He didn't care whether
the hound belonged to King Richard's men or to the other side, or whether it was
simply a wild creature, nothing was going to harm Chloe, not while Winnie had breath
on his body.

He was just in the nick of time and, as the great beast crouched ready to spring, he
hurled himself on to its haunches and sank his sharp claws and teeth into its flesh.
It let out a howl of pain and rage
and leapt backwards, spinning
in the air, to confront Winnie,
who had let go and puffed up
all his fur so he looked three
times his normal size. Winnie
hissed and yowled and bared
his own fangs, as if to say, 'OK
Buster, I'm ready!'

But at that moment the
hound's gaze fell upon the cap with
its tantalising contents of fresh fish
and shrimps and hermit crabs.

He was emanating this brilliant blue light.

'Oh no!' Winnie screamed. 'Don't take my cap! DON'T TAKE MY CAP!'

'If you don't give it to me, I'll eat *you* – BOTH OF YOU – and the stupid cap as well!' the enormous dog growled. 'I'm *starving*!'

'You're welcome to the fish, kind sir,' Chloe said sweetly, realising that a bit of gentle female persuasion was their safest bet. 'My friend here is very fond of his cap but of course he will happily give you the fish to eat...'

Winnie shot out his paw and tipped the entire contents of his beloved cap on to the nearest rock, whereupon the dog, who was clearly starving, dived into it and started greedily munching and crunching with his sharp teeth. 'Oh well, there goes our dinner,' Winnie thought, 'but at least I've still got my magic cap!'

'Come on, Chloe!' he said. 'He'll finish that in 20 seconds and I don't fancy being his dessert...' And he grabbed her paw and once again they were tearing off but this time back in the direction of the battlefield. 'He won't want to follow us into that lot!' Winnie said, clasping her paw even more tightly. 'It's time for us to join the fray!'

And before she had time to think, Chloe was half-running, half being pulled along towards the battlefield. Gasping for breath, she and Winnie quickly found themselves having to dodge arrows and horses' hooves as well as the big clod-hopping feet of the soldiers on the ground who were clashing and bashing at each other with their swords.

'Stop!' Chloe begged. 'I can't run any further, Winnie – *please* can we stop just for a moment...?'

'No! It's not safe here!' Winnie replied, picking her up and continuing to run on his back legs, just like a snuzzle! 'Wow! How come I can do that?!' he gasped under his breath. 'This is Magic!' And he ran as fast as his two back legs would take him while Chloe hung on for dear life with both her front paws wrapped so tightly around his neck that Winnie thought he would choke.

But then, away to the right, he spotted a mound of earth – an ants' nest which he reckoned was just big enough for them to hide behind – and a moment later the two moggies were flat on their backs huffing and puffing, but safely out of sight.

As they gradually got their breath back they rolled over on to their tummies again and peeped over the top of the mound. Now that they were so much closer to the action, they could see which men belonged to King Richard and which to the Emperor Isaac. They could see that more of Isaac's men had horses so they had the advantage. And they could also tell that the few horses belonging to King Richard's men were tired from all their weeks of tossing about on the stormy sea.

'It's not fair!' Winnie said. 'The only reason they're fighting at all is because that crafty Isaac treated Richard's girlfriend so rudely and now Richard has to take part in this stupid battle...'

'But he will win, won't he?' Chloe asked. 'I mean, we know that he did win...'

'I'm not sure,' Winnie said. 'We've gone back in time and I don't think we were here the first time this battle was fought so maybe everything really is different now which means that, oh dear, maybe our King Richard will lose – maybe even get killed – and then, oh no, what will happen to his girlfriend Berengaria who's waiting out there in one of those ships?'

'We've got to *do* something!' Chloe said, suddenly feeling strong and brave – not at all like her usual timid self.

'But what *can* we do?' Winnie sighed. 'We're just a couple of moggies on a snuzzle battlefield 800 years before we've even been born... It makes my mind boggle and I can't think straight...'

'Well I *can* think straight!' Chloe said firmly, 'and we are *not* "just a couple of moggies"... Only a few moments ago *you* said cats can do anything! Also, because I only have one eye which means I have to work a lot harder to see clearly, I actually notice things that others might miss!'

And at that very moment she did indeed see something that others might have missed – two things, in fact:

As she had been watching the fighting, she had noticed that one of the English soldiers had a vibrant blue light shooting out of his shoulders. At first she had thought she was imagining things but she had quickly realised that, no, there really was something different about that one soldier. Not only was he emanating this brilliant blue light but he also seemed to be in three places at once. It seemed as if nothing could stop him as he flailed his battleaxe and shouted at the enemy soldiers ganging up on him.

'Winnie! That must be King Richard!' she said with a thrill in her voice. 'After everything you told me in the castle about his bravery in battle and his lack of fear in the face of death, don't you agree it has to be him?!'

'Yes, I do!' Winnie said excitedly.

'And can you see the blue light?'

'Yes, I can! And look – it's getting brighter and stronger and it's shooting out of his sword and battleaxe as well.'

But even though it was true that the King was fighting with the heart and strength of a lion, it was also true that he desperately needed a horse. Winnie and Chloe could see that he was in great danger, being down on the ground while so many of Emperor Isaac's soldiers were on horseback and could easily attack him or even knock him over and trample him under their horses' hooves. What a terrible thought!

And then, as if to prove to them that their fears were well-founded, they saw three enemy soldiers on their enormous horses approaching Richard from behind. Richard couldn't see them because he was so intent on fighting two other footsoldiers in front of him... Both moggies held their breath.

And it was then that Chloe saw the second thing: a horse which had lost its rider was standing in a state of fear and confusion just a few yards away.

'Quick, Winnie! Magnetise...!'

This is a command which every moggy on the planet understands. It is the power they use in their own battles and when they are hunting and so Winnie immediately knew what they must do.

The two moggies turned their unflinching gaze directly on the loose horse, and their combined magnetic power was so great that the horse immediately got the message and headed straight towards the struggling King. Chloe and Winnie then turned their attention to two of Richard's own men and, in a trice, the horse was at Richard's side and the two powerful men had hoisted him up and into the saddle.

'Next time you won't be so quick to say we're "just a couple of moggies", will you?!' Chloe laughed.

'No, I won't! We're FAN-TAS-TIC!'

'Of course we are!' Chloe agreed. 'We always have been and we always will! Now we can feel much more confident that King Richard will prevail...'

But as the words were leaving her mouth and they were just beginning to duck back down behind the ant hill, something that neither of them could have imagined in their wildest, craziest dreams happened.

'Quick! Up here!' came a powerful voice and, as our two adventurers looked up, they found themselves staring straight into the King's face from where he sat astride the magnificent beast. 'I will always be in your debt!' he shouted above the battle noise. 'You haven't *changed* history, this is exactly how it was – or, should I say, exactly how it *is*... Everything will be explained to you later but now we haven't a moment to lose!'

And instantly the two soldiers who had helped their King to mount the massive warhorse grabbed Chloe and Winnie by the scruffs of their necks and hurled them unceremoniously on to the horse, behind the King. They scrabbled madly to hang on and eventually managed to dig their claws deep into the leather saddle.

'Good work!' the King shouted over his shoulder, casting his battleaxe to the ground and unsheathing his sword. 'This is going to be fun!'

Chloe wasn't certain she would have described the next three hours as 'fun' but it certainly was the greatest, most adventurous experience of her whole life. And of course, for Winnie, it *was* fun. True, it was very dangerous and also very hard work trying to hang on as the horse galloped here and there, this way and that, rearing up when they least expected it, and the King plunging in and out of first one fray and then another, but, oh yes, it was right up Winnie's street!

But just when Winnie had decided he had never had so much fun in all his life and that this snuzzle-fighting was a very entertaining game, things suddenly got Very Serious Indeed. They had got used to the lunging and rearing of the horse – it reminded Winnie of being at sea with Plug when The Courageous Sea-Cat was being tossed about in a storm – but this time there was something very different going on. Instead of just rearing right up and then plunging down towards the ground, this time the horse was plunging down *sideways.* Oh no! Winnie and Chloe both realised at the very same moment that the horse was *falling!* Not only that, but no fewer than four enemy soldiers had seen what was happening and were getting ready to encircle the horse in order to... Oh, it was better not to think about what they might do once the horse had fallen and the King and Winnie and Chloe were all scrambling about helplessly on the ground...

'This *is* mortal danger!' Winnie thought. 'If ever the time was right for my magic golden thread, it's NOW!' And, hanging on even tighter to the King's saddle as the horse fell heavily towards the ground, he reached up and touched the magic golden thread in his cap and with all his might he cried out for Loulou's help.

Everything seemed to happen in slow motion. The enormous weight of the King's armour and shield were making it almost impossible for him to keep himself in the saddle as the great horse keeled over; the four menacing footsoldiers were marching forwards with their swords drawn and vicious expressions on their faces which reminded Winnie of Jezza and his criminal mates; Chloe slid right down so that she was hanging by just one claw and was in danger of being crushed by the horse when it hit the ground; and Winnie came within a whisker of dropping his precious cap into the dirt as he reached for the thread which he hoped and prayed would save their lives.

He looked up into the late afternoon sky, not knowing what to expect. There were a few dark clouds around, hiding the sun, and this made the atmosphere seem even more threatening. His heart sank as an even darker thundercloud appeared overhead. This was the last straw because, like all cats, big and small, Winnie and Chloe were afraid of thunder – much more afraid of thunder than of the battle.

But wait! Winnie craned his neck up, up, up and, Yes! It wasn't a thundercloud at all, it was the carpet! Loulou *had* heard them! Help was at hand! And with an almighty whooshing sound the carpet dived down towards the ground and in the twinkling of an eye and at the very last second before the horse would have hit the ground, it had scooped them all up – the horse and the King, as well as Winnie and Chloe – and they were now zooming up into the sky, high above the battlefield, at breakneck speed, leaving the four bloodthirsty soldiers staring up into heaven, unable to believe their eyes. It seemed that God Himself had plucked their enemy from right under their noses and they fell to their knees in fear.

'Welcome aboard, one and all!' King Richard cried, holding on tight to the horse's bridle. 'Now we will have great sport!' And his eyes flashed and he gave a hearty laugh as the carpet bucked and jolted beneath them. 'My dear friend, Derrashah,' he called out to Loulou. 'We meet again! Just like old times, eh?! What adventures we have had, you and I, over all these centuries! And now our great minds blend once more so that a mighty victory will soon be ours!'

And Winnie saw how Loulou smiled and bowed and looked young again. The young co-pilot could hardly believe it. Loulou actually *knew* King Richard the Lionheart! Wow! What a day this was turning out to be! He desperately wanted to know the whole story but this was not the moment, far from it...

For now the carpet was plummeting back towards the Earth, just beyond where the battle between the thunderstruck soldiers was taking place. It slowed just in time to hover a few inches from the ground so that the King could let the terrified horse (which had been staggering about on the carpet, almost wishing he was back in the boat on the stormy sea) leap safely down with a whinny of relief.

'I will come for you later,' said the King, giving the horse an affectionate slap on its bum. 'You have served me well this day and I will not forget it.'

With that, he gave Loulou the signal to instruct the carpet to follow the King's commands from now on and they were soon back in the thick of it.

For once, Winnie found himself silent and still, watching in awe as time and again the carpet dived downwards and King Richard, with great glee, walloped the enemy from above. He was so magnificent that Winnie briefly didn't even consider showing off. The Lionheart leapt and lunged this way and that across the carpet, knocking the enemy off their horses with the butt end of his sword and roaring with laughter as they tumbled down in ungainly heaps.

'No need to kill them!' he shouted above the din. 'They will soon admit defeat. So in the meantime I'm just going to enjoy myself! Come on, young Winnie!' he called over

his shoulder. 'Surely, *you* remember the last time you were here as well?!'

Me?! Winnie muttered to himself, trying to pull himself together.

'Certainly, young sire!' replied the King, reading his thoughts. 'Nothing is new! We have all been here before, all of us together – including the dear ladies...' And he turned his head in the direction of the far end of the carpet where Winnie could now see that Hissie and Sylvester were also aboard and that they were embracing Chloe as old friends. Winnie shook his head, trying to make sense of it all, but then he decided to give up and just enjoy the action.

'Ahoy there!' came a familiar voice just behind him.

'Plug!' Winnie cried with a mixture of delight and embarrassment, remembering that it was because of him that poor old Plug had been coshed on the head outside The Cat's Whiskers just a few hours ago. 'Oh, Plug, I'm *such* a twit and I'm *so so* sorry!'

'No real harm done, my lad,' Plug said kindly. 'Follow me!'

And he led Winnie to the very edge of the carpet where they lay down flat on their tummies, their noses peeking through the golden tassels so they could get an uninterrupted view of the battlefield below.

'There goes the Emperor!' they heard Richard cry with a laugh of contempt, 'heading for the hills!'

And, sure enough, they could make out the figure of Isaac hanging on to his horse for dear life and spurring it on to greater and greater speed as far away from Richard as he could go. They chased him just for fun and Winnie found himself giggling hysterically as the carpet swooped and plunged over the fleeing coward so that Richard could give him little prods with his sword – not so as to knock him off his horse, just enough to give him the jitters.

'Enough!' the King cried. 'One final assault and we can count the day as ours.'

And they returned to the battlefield, the carpet expanding to the size of a tennis court, and Winnie could barely see to the other side where Hissie, Chloe and Sylvester were hanging on to each other. The terrifying sight of the massive bucking carpet growing in size and hurling itself in their direction was more than the remaining enemy soldiers could stand. They threw their weapons to the ground and, crying out for mercy, raced after their fleeing Emperor, and headed for the distant hills instead of returning to their camp.

'Very well, men!' the King shouted as the carpet settled back down on to the churned-up earth. 'Help yourselves to the booty! There should be plenty to be had!' And he laughed again as his men cheered and hurried off as fast as their legs or their horses could carry them to help themselves to the riches which Isaac's soldiers and camp followers had left in their haste: gold plate

and jewelled buckles and warm blankets and embroidered jackets and much much more – and of course gallons and gallons of strong red wine.

Richard laughed again: 'They will be dead drunk before the hour is out! But they will be safe sleeping it off here, the enemy will not dare return.'

And then, as if by magic (and of course it *was* Magic), a soothing amethyst mist descended over the carpet and everything went quiet and still and peaceful and Winnie found himself feeling very very drowsy.

'That's right,' he heard the King say softly. 'We need a brief period of replenishment before our next task.'

And Winnie's chin sank down on his chest and his co-pilot's cap slipped over his eyes and soon he was sound asleep. And yet it didn't *feel* like sleep, not exactly. He felt as if he were in a delicious bed of flower petals and all his favourite friends – including his newest friend Miss Chloe – were gathered around him, stroking his brow and telling him that nobody was cross with him and explaining to him that here in this magic place, Time all happened at once so that, yes, it was the year 1191 but it was also every year and every minute in between right up to Now. It was all Now. And somehow, in his fuzzy magical sleep, it all made perfect sense to Winnie so that, when a few minutes later he was waking up again, feeling perfectly refreshed and renewed, he didn't think there was anything peculiar about King Richard's next words:

'Off we go once more! See how the storm has passed and the sea beneath us is like a turquoise mirror! And see how my ships on the horizon are resting steadily at anchor waiting for us. For, yes, now we are going to rescue my fair Berengaria and bring her safely back to Limassol Castle where we shall be wed and I shall crown her Queen!'

At this, everyone cheered and the ladies all sighed and smiled soppy smiles.

'And all of you, my beloved friends of old, you will be our honoured guests at the wedding banquet. And we shall sing together and tell stories and share our happiness – and remind ourselves that, while all these extraordinary details have been left out of the modern snuzzle history books, the truth is that without the heroic Malekidi Moggies and their wondrous magic carpet, the story of King Richard the Lionheart would have been very different indeed. I owe you my life, my victory and my eternal gratitude! And I can tell you now that we will meet again and again and again over the centuries that lie before us and what times we shall have!'

And everyone cheered again, none more loudly than Winnie who had regained all his verve and bounce and was ready for anything.

As the carpet sped out towards the ships on the horizon, the Malekidi Moggies were each lost in their own thoughts. Loulou was casting his mind back over all the centuries he and Richard had stood shoulder to shoulder; and Winnie was imagining far into the future and all the amazing adventures that must surely still lie ahead; and Plug was chewing on a piece of catnip tobacco and chuckling to himself; and Sylvester was longing to dive into the crystal clear water and swim like her Uncle Van; and Hissie was thinking how romantic it would be to be a princess being rescued by a brave King; and Miss Chloe simply stared into space, asking herself if this was really truly happening or whether the whole thing was an extraordinary dream.

But in less than three minutes they were all jerked out of their reveries because the carpet was already hovering over the largest of the ships with its great sails billowing in the breeze and all was activity and excitement.

King Richard beckoned to Loulou, his wise counsellor, to accompany him as he wished to discuss the wedding with him. Winnie was delighted to be told he could go anywhere he wanted on the whole ship and so he set off at high speed to explore all

the exciting nooks and crannies and, in no time at all, he was best friends with Jack and Jake, the ship's cats.

Meanwhile, Hissie, Chloe and Sylvester were led by a smiling lady-in-waiting to sit with Berengaria, whom they discovered to be a delightful and quiet lady who talked to them in a gentle voice and gave them little titbits of shrimp as they purred at her feet. They thought of King Richard and how tall he was and how fair his hair and how blue his eyes, and how swashbuckling and noisy he liked to be – almost like Winnie – and how very small and elegant and calm Berengaria was, with her shiny dark hair and deep brown eyes. And Hissie and Chloe whispered together about how romantic it was, and Sylvester just giggled and winked and tucked into the shrimps.

And then, once again, a great sleepiness overcame them so that the next thing any of them knew was that they were in a small stone chapel which was filled with magnificently dressed snuzzles of every description and the air was heavy with the scent of incense. To be honest, our moggy-friends didn't like the incense much. With their keen sense of smell, it was overpowering but none of them was going to let that spoil the moment. They knew in their bones that something very important was about to happen and Chloe suddenly felt cold and afraid, although she wasn't sure why. What *was* it that had spooked her? And, as if reading her thoughts, Winnie put his paw around her shoulder and said:

'Don't worry Miss Chloe, you're only feeling anxious because you recognise that we are back in Limassol Castle again... But you're quite safe this time, those horrible criminals are hundreds of years into the future and here we both are as the honoured guests of a King and his soon-to-be-crowned Queen!'

'Oh yes!' Chloe exclaimed. 'That was it. My whiskers and my sense of smell told me that this was a place of danger but now I see that it is a place of great celebration. Oh Winnie, aren't we lucky!'

King Richard had made sure that all the moggies were seated near the front so they could see everything clearly and even Winnie remembered to keep quiet as he sat up tall and straight on his cushion.

There was a loud blast from a strange musical instrument that looked a bit like the bagpipes, and ten men started blowing on wooden flutes while another lot jingled silver bells. It was a very merry sound and then a great cheer went up as King Richard, dressed in a tunic of red and gold, strode into the chapel. He had a gold-hilted sword in a silver scabbard around his waist and a jewelled crown upon his golden hair and he smiled broadly as he reached out his hand to greet Berengaria who approached from the other side of the chapel.

Although she was so small and dark compared with the bridegroom, she shone with a gentle radiance which touched everybody there (even Winnie). She wore a gown of jade green velvet and a rich girdle sparkling with gemstones and her dark hair was long and loose and flowing to her shoulders.

Hissie, Sylvester, Chloe, Winnie and Plug were unfamiliar with snuzzle wedding ceremonies and were most relieved that this one turned out to be short because they were still hungry and, above the heady smell of the incense which they didn't like at all, they could smell delicious cooking smells coming from somewhere beyond the chapel in preparation for the feasting that would soon take place.

But they weren't to get off quite that lightly because, no sooner had Richard placed the wedding ring upon Berengaria's finger and the chaplain had pronounced them man and wife, than two Bishops and an Archbishop, all done up in long embroidered robes and golden pointy hats, stepped forward to crown Richard, King of Cyprus, and Berengaria, in her turn, Queen of both Cyprus and England. Richard, of course, was already King of England and it was he who placed the crown on Berengaria's head and then, holding her hand, he called out to the whole assembled company to greet their new Queen, his bride.

And the chapel erupted and the walls shook as every snuzzle present shouted in unison, 'Vivat Regina!' which is old Latin for 'Long live the Queen!'

The noise was so loud – much louder than anything Winnie had ever heard at The Cat's Whiskers – that all the moggies (except dignified Loulou of course) clapped their paws over

Their new Queen,
his bride

their ears and screwed up their faces and, even though it was probably very rude, made a mad dash for the door so that the moment it was opened they all tumbled out of the hot and stuffy chapel and into the Big Hall where the great feast had been laid out.

This was more like it! Because, even though Hissie and Chloe had enjoyed the romance of the wedding, they had to agree with Winnie and Sylvester that the idea of a banquet and a bit of space to run about in was much more appealing than having to be quiet and serious during the church service.

And they weren't disappointed. Not only was the food more sumptuous than anything they had ever seen in all their lives, but it was so entertaining to watch the richly clothed snuzzles getting more and more tipsy, so that their dancing, which was very elegant at the beginning, became more and more unsteady and outrageous, with some of them falling over in great heaps amid gales of laughter. It was all very colourful and jolly good fun.

It won't surprise you to hear that Winnie couldn't resist joining in rather more energetically than the ladies and Loulou did, but nobody got cross with him as he darted in and out amongst the snuzzles' legs and tore at great speed all the way up the heavy tapestry wall-hanging at the far end of the hall, and once he even leapt right on to the banqueting table and darted off with a whole lobster which was almost as big as he was.

'I think that's enough,' said Loulou quietly in Winnie's ear, sidling up beside the young rascal. 'Everyone finds you very amusing but I know you too well and at this rate it won't be long before you do something TOO naughty and then you might be back in the soup, so to speak... You are, after all, the guest of a very powerful King... *Do you understand?*'

Winnie could detect the tone in Loulou's voice which let him know, loud and clear, that it was time to calm down.

'Yes, Loulou,' he said, still panting from all his exertions. 'I'll be good now...'

'I'm very glad to hear it,' said Loulou in a pretend-serious voice. 'I must go back to the King's side now because, look, he is about to make a speech.'

Sure enough, King Richard had risen from his place at the head of the banqueting table and was starting to speak. Actually, moggies don't usually find snuzzle speeches very interesting and they tend to curl up and go to sleep at such times – especially when their tummies are filled to bursting with delicious treats. But just as they were all beginning to feel very snoozy, they were jolted back into wakefulness by something amazing the King was saying:

'My dear friends, ladies and gentlemen, companions in arms – I salute you all but there are among us this evening six especially welcome and valued guests whom I wish to honour on this happy occasion.'

Even the tipsiest of the guests were now as quiet as mice as the King stood tall and still, smiling down first at his bride and then at Loulou at his side. 'I refer of course to the legendary Malekidi Moggies who have played such a vital part in our victory today and who have graced us with their presence – and, in the case of one of their number, their entertaining antics!'

All eyes swivelled towards Winnie who was blushing from the tip of his nose to the tip of his tail, and everyone laughed and clapped and cheered.

'First of all, I wish to bestow the Order of the Huggable Heroine on Miss Chloe Cuddlebucket, who will henceforth be known as *DAME* Chloe Cuddlebucket...!'

'*ME?*' Chloe gasped in disbelief, shaking with a mixture of excitement and anxiety. 'What have I done...?'

'You, madam,' the King said in a ringing voice, 'have demonstrated one of the greatest of all strengths. Ever since you were locked up in this very place and even though you are naturally rather a nervous lady, you have shown that it is possible to KEEP YOUR HEAD IN A CRISIS! This is a truly great quality and I salute you!' And he stepped forward and bent to slip a gold medallion on a pink satin ribbon over Chloe's head. She managed to perform a dainty curtsy, before fainting clean away into Winnie's arms.

'Next we come to the ladies Hissie and Sylvester,' the King continued. 'Upon you I bestow the Order of the Prawn Cocktail for you have so often taken it upon yourselves to provide food for your male comrades and, as I know all too well, armies can achieve NOTHING if they are not well fed. You have created culinary delicacies, often at a moment's notice, for more centuries then you can remember and we all bow to you...'

And they, too, received gold medallions on pink satin ribbons.

'And now for an invaluable member of any ship's crew,' Richard continued with a grin and a twinkle in his eye. 'Who do we need on board to make sure our victuals are kept safe? Who do we need to make sure we do not lose our precious supplies to the scourge of all seafaring folk? I am, of course, referring to every sailor's friend, the ship's cat, who earns our gratitude by keeping vermin at bay! And who is the noblest, most experienced and beloved of all such ocean-going moggies? Why, Mr Plug himself, the one and only!'

And as everybody turned their heads, Plug bounded forwards, looking as scruffily magnificent as ever, wearing his battle scars with pride and punching his fists in the air and bowing from side to side as he approached his King and knelt before him.

'I declare you Admiral Horatio Plug,' Richard announced in a booming voice. 'I grant you this honour in memory of a famous snuzzle, Admiral Horatio Nelson, whom I have often met on the Timeless Planet and with whom I have had many interesting discussions about battle strategy. This Admiral Nelson also sported a manly eye-patch for he, too, had lost an eye in the course of duty.' And he tapped Plug's head three times with the tip of his gold-handled dagger and presented Plug with a magnificent new eye-patch made from black velvet trimmed with gold braid.

And, as the applause died down, the King grinned broadly and said: 'I will now surprise you all! Because we must also honour our so-called enemies – who, in truth,

Admiral Plug, are not our enemies at all – I bestow the Order of the Righteous Rodent on that great adversary of yours, mighty Hercules!' And to everyone's amazement and with a great scuffling sound, Hercules (whom Winnie remembered so well from his days at sea on The Courageous Sea Cat) scurried across the floor, chuckling to himself and playfully tugging at Plug's tail, to receive his award before scampering away again and disappearing through a mouse hole that looked far too small for his fat tummy.

'And upon you, young man,' the King smiled, turning to Winnie and looking even taller than he really was, 'there is a very special honour I wish to declare. For you are a Daredevil – a man after my own heart – and, just as armies can achieve nothing if they are not well fed, so they can achieve nothing without the Daredevils to inspire them with new resolve and new courage. I know much more about you than you might realise and I saw how you protected Miss Chloe and tried to calm her fears during her Great Ordeal which I have already mentioned. And for this, I declare that I shall share with you the title which has been given to me myself and you are henceforth to be known as Winnie the Lionheart!'

The eruption of cheering and applause that followed was almost as loud as that in the chapel earlier but this time none of the moggies clapped their paws over their ears because they themselves were cheering so loudly and slapping their beloved young co-pilot on the back as he stepped forward to receive his award. And this time, instead of a medallion on a ribbon, King Richard pinned a golden heart-shaped badge on the front of Winnie's co-pilot's cap, where it gleamed and shone almost as much as Winnie himself. He was the proudest young man in the whole Universe.

But now the King was raising his hand for silence and he turned with great reverence and respect to face Loulou who had been seated upright all this time on a tall golden stool with a purple cushion. And it was with near disbelief that everyone noticed a tear running down the King's cheek as he began to speak:

'All of you here present,' he declared, 'look upon this noble Being! Just as armies are nothing if they are not well fed and if they do not have Daredevils to inspire them, so, more than anything else, they are NOTHING without wise advisers! Oh Great Loulou – known by the Great Ones as Derrashah – how many times over all these centuries has your wise counsel saved my skin! Time and again you have curbed my wilder impulses so as to ensure success in all my endeavours and I can never express my gratitude sufficiently. In many different guises, in many different and often incredible situations, we have stood shoulder to shoulder and no doubt we shall do so many a time again in the glorious future that lies ahead. I know that Winnie the Lionheart and Admiral Plug and these magnificent ladies, Hissie, Sylvester, and Dame Chloe Cuddlebucket will join with all this company as I declare you, my Great Counsellor and Adviser, to be for ever hailed as Lord Loulou of Limassol!'

And this time, not only did the King bestow a magnificent medallion on a scarlet ribbon around Lord Loulou's neck and drape an emerald green shawl of the finest silk around his shoulders, but he embraced him as if he were his dearest friend and closest companion, which in truth he was.

There were tears on the cheeks of everyone present – tears of joy and pride as they allowed themselves to remember all the highs and lows of the swashbuckling campaigns they had fought over the centuries.

'And there is only one more thing I would like to say before I retire for the evening with my bride and leave you all to enjoy your dancing and rejoicing – and your drinking! And that is this: there is a great historic parallel between Winnie the Lionheart's rescue of the courageous Dame Chloe and my own rescue of my fair Berengaria... We would all do well to raise our chalices to these two brave ladies, both caught up and terrorised by the stupidity and greed of MEN!'

It was impossible to tell which was louder, the cheers which came in response to the King's wisdom and regal bearing or the laughter in response to his good humour as he swept from the room with his Queen on his arm.

And then everything seemed to happen very quickly and all at once. The musicians struck up on their instruments; the richly dressed snuzzles linked hands and started dancing in circles; more silver platters piled high with every imaginable delicacy were carried into the chamber and laid out upon the massive table; Winnie and Plug danced a hornpipe together; Sylvester and Hissie were twirled about by tall handsome sailors until they were quite breathless; and six tumblers performed a breathtaking display, leaping over the tables and the revellers and balancing, sometimes with only one hand, on the golden thrones where the King and Queen had so recently sat.

And in a brief lull while everyone was getting their breath back, Admiral Horatio Plug approached Dame Chloe Cuddlebucket, bowed low with his smart new eye-patch glinting in the candlelight, and said in a deep voice:

'You and I are members of a very special clan – the Clan of the Single-Eyed Sages

– and so we have a deep affinity with each other and I ask you to do me the honour of performing with me a dance I learnt while serving on a ship in Argentina...' And, despite her wonky legs, Chloe found herself performing a perfect tango as the ruggedly handsome old sea-cat swept her along so that her paws hardly touched the ground. And everyone looked on in amazement because, you see, the tango hadn't been invented in 1191 and everyone found it rather thrilling – especially Dame Chloe herself.

And because everybody's attention was absorbed by this new spectacle, nobody noticed Lord Loulou as he silently raised his paw and whispered a powerful ancient incantation under his breath – an incantation so secret and so sacred that I'm not allowed to write it here...

It was Winnie who first noticed that a strange mist had begun to descend upon the room and he couldn't work out what was happening. And then all at once there was a massive flash of the brightest lightning you could ever imagine and in the twinkling of an eye all the Malekidi Moggies, including Plug and Chloe, found themselves floating silently upwards on their faithful old carpet, as if emerging from a dream.

'What's *happening*?!' cried Winnie. 'Where *is* everybody?!'

'Yes,' agreed Plug. 'That was rather sudden!'

And the three ladies chimed in together, 'Yes, Loulou, where *are* we? And where are we going? And what's happened to all the snuzzles...?'

'I'll explain in a minute!' Loulou replied. 'But now, come to the edge and look down... Look! There's King Richard! See? – down *there*!'

And, sure enough, as they peered over the edge of the fabulous carpet, there was King Richard, a long way below them, calling out to them and holding his sword aloft in a very kingly manner.

'Farewell, Your Majesty!' they all called back, waving their arms wildly about and hoping that the solitary figure below could see them.

And then they were high above the clouds and all was peaceful and every one of them was stunned into silence by the suddenness of their departure.

Had it all really *happened*, they wondered? Of course it had! And yet, they couldn't get their heads around it.

'Have we been gone for five minutes or for 800 years?' Winnie asked.

'And are we still the same Malekidi Moggies we always were?' Sylvester and Hissie asked themselves.

'And was I *really* kidnapped?' thought Miss Chloe.

'The answer to all your questions is, Yes,' came Loulou's strong clear voice. 'We are all the same Malekidi Moggies and we have been together in countless adventures over countless centuries all over the world and beyond the world. And we shall continue for ever and ever. But we have been given a great gift this day because we have been allowed to return to a former life to experience one of our greatest adventures all over again and so, perhaps, from now on we will indeed be a little bit changed...'

'So that's why when you told me the story of the Snuzzle King when I was a kitten,' said Winnie, 'it seemed so real! You had already been there, Loulou – and I had been there too!'

'Yes!' Loulou said with a smile. 'But did you notice how quickly Time seemed to pass? When we were with King Richard 800 years ago, those battles lasted over many weeks, not merely the few hours it has seemed to us today. When you go back and live things over again Time compresses itself... It has to! Just think – if the memories took as long as the original events, you would never have time to live your life Now!'

'But Loulou,' Winnie said with a worried look on his face, 'I understand that, in some magical way, *you* remember everything that has ever happened to you but *I* didn't remember any of it before we went there again...'

'That's true,' Loulou agreed. 'All of us here are very ancient moggies but I am the most ancient of us all and that is why I remember – and also why I sleep a lot because, in sleeping, the remembering becomes clearer. And one day, Winnie, young man, you will be as ancient as I am today and you will find yourself sleeping a lot and remembering more and more and being able to share it with youngsters who want to hear your stories or who need to be calmed when they have had a nightmare, just as you needed to be calmed when you were a kitten.'

'I understand, Loulou, but you *must* tell us the rest of the story! You pulled us away from that big party and we don't know what happened next!'

'That will have to wait for another day,' said Loulou mysteriously. 'But one thing I *can* tell you is that that old villain Isaac – the one who tried to capture Berengaria and defeat Richard – was treated well by the Lionheart... And that's another important lesson – we must learn to be merciful when we are victorious. That is the sign of a great snuzzle – and it is just as true in our moggy world...

'But being merciful doesn't mean you have to be *stupid*! Quick, look over there..!' And he raised his paw and pointed over the clouds.

'Oh my!' Miss Chloe said in a shocked voice. 'It's those horrible ruffians, Jezza and his mates, the ones who threatened to kill me!'

'And there's Minnie the Mouser!' Winnie joined in. 'AND The Hoodlum!'

'They're not coming this way, are they?' asked Chloe, Hissie and Sylvester all at the same time.

'No, don't worry,' Loulou assured them. 'But keep your eyes open – there's going to be quite a show!'

And no sooner had he stopped speaking than a dazzling white tornado whirled across the sky, sucking all the criminals right into its centre, just like a massive hoover, before whirling away again with a deafening roar until it was completely out of sight.

'Where have they gone?' Winnie asked.

'And will they come back?' Chloe asked with a shudder. 'I know you talked about being merciful to people who haven't been nice to us, Loulou, but I really wouldn't like to meet any of them again...'

Loulou smiled. 'I also said we mustn't be stupid, didn't I? So the answer to both of you is that, No, they won't ever be back because they have been blasted on to another planet in another dimension where they will be perfectly happy because the whole planet is full of crooks just like themselves!'

'Yesssss!' shouted Winnie, punching his fists in the air and jumping up and down. 'Wheeeee!'

And Lord Loulou simply raised his eyebrows, shook his head and sighed, 'I think it's time we all went home, don't you?'

The next couple of hours passed in a whirl of happiness and magic. Jezza's gang and Minnie the Mouser and The Hoodlum had been blasted out of their lives forever and they all stretched out in the sunshine and stared at the fluffy white clouds, each lost in their own thoughts. And then all of a sudden they were once again floating gently along The Molos, the beautiful beachfront esplanade in Limassol where Winnie had first met Plug.

'Just one small detour,' Loulou announced and, instead of heading straight to Malekidi Street, the carpet sailed gently along for a mile or so until Chloe suddenly clapped her paws together and cried, 'Oh, look! There's my balcony! I'm home!'

'Yes,' said Loulou, as the carpet hovered gently on a level with the balcony of Chloe's fourth-floor flat. As they all peered over the edge of the rug, they could see through the big glass doors into the living room where Valerie Snuzzle was sitting in a chair, holding a cup of tea and looking very sadly at a picture of Chloe on the table.

'Quick!' Loulou said in a loud whisper. 'Go on, Chloe – hop on to the balcony and then *very quietly* go into the living room and sit where she'll be able to see you when she turns round, and then give a gentle little meow... You want to give her a lovely surprise, not a terrible shock, so whatever you do don't go straight in and jump on her lap!'

'As if I would!' Chloe said, winking her one eye and pretending to be indignant. But she couldn't pretend very well because she was so happy to be home and couldn't wait to see the look on Valerie's face.

'Off you go then,' said Hissie and Sylvester in unison, while Winnie and Plug gave her the thumbs-up and Loulou smiled encouragingly. 'We'll be friends for ever,' he said. 'Dame Chloe, you are now an official Malekidi Moggy!'

They waited a few moments – just long enough to see the look of disbelief and joy flood over Valerie's face as she scooped her beloved missing moggy into her arms and burst into happy tears. Chloe snuggled up as close as she could and just managed to wave one paw at her friends outside the window as they flew off towards Number 9 Malekidi Street, their own Home Sweet Home.

The news had spread far and wide that all the criminals had been soundly defeated by the courage and cleverness of the Malekidi Moggies and everyone at The Cat's Whiskers was thrilled that the bungled kidnapping had not resulted in tragedy. Big Mamma insisted that all of them, including Hissie and Sylvester who would never normally have been seen in such a place as The Cat's Whiskers, must join her for the evening and that all their food and drink would be paid for and the band would play all their favourite tunes – the sea shanties which Plug loved; the traditional jazz beloved of Loulou; the soppy love songs favoured by Hissie; the noisy headbanging so-called 'music' which Winnie was addicted to; and the Turkish folk songs which Sylvester had learned from her Uncle Van.

Everybody wanted to congratulate them and everybody wanted to know the whole story and they gathered round, eager to catch every word. But the odd thing was that even though Winnie, Hissie, Sylvester and Plug kept having vague, misty memories of strange battles and horses and glamorous snuzzles, and other dreamlike visions, they found that, when they tried to put them all together in their heads, they disappeared like moonshine.

Only Loulou, the wise old counsellor, could remember exactly what had happened in that time-travelling adventure with Richard the Lionheart. It was he, magical Loulou, who had kindly and quietly removed these memories from the minds of his younger moggy friends. He knew only too well that, if they could remember everything from lifetime to lifetime to lifetime, it would scramble their brains. And he smiled to himself as he thought of how Winnie would have swaggered about even more than usual if he could tell people he was best friends with the courageous Snuzzle King, Richard the Lionheart!

It was enough that they could remember everything that had happened in the earthly dimension – the kidnap, Winnie and Chloe's ordeal in the castle, the last-minute rescue on the magic carpet and the blasting of the criminals into outer space. That was quite enough of a story in itself!

However, they did still have the gifts which had been presented to them by the King and when they questioned him about these, Loulou explained it thus:

'Whenever a moggy performs some particularly dangerous or demanding service, I am permitted to conjure an appropriate reward and this is what I have done because all of you have indeed given great service this day.' He paused for a moment and then added:

'There is just one other thing I would like to say. I was ready to be very cross with our young Winnie here for so foolishly keeping from us the truth about that dangerous Dare he had taken on with Minnie the Mouser and The Hoodlum. He could have saved himself a great deal of anguish and life-threatening danger, if he had come and told us the truth in the first place...'

For a moment Loulou looked extremely stern and everyone held their breath. 'HOWEVER,' he continued, changing his frown to a broad smile, 'if he *had* told us the truth, he would never have ended up in the Castle and he would never have discovered Miss Chloe, and the ending would have been a very tragic one... And so, young man, I completely and absolutely exonerate you from all blame and I ask you all to raise your glasses to young Winnie – with one final command:

'Don't you EVER do anything so STUPID again!'

And everyone cheered and everyone laughed, and Winnie the Lionheart was so happy that he did a double somersault right over the bar.

HISSIE'S HAPPY HOLIDAY

The next morning, Loulou was up and about before sunrise, just as he always was. He sniffed the air and looked over to where Winnie was lying on his back with his legs flopped apart and his co-pilot's cap down over his nose, all skew-whiff. Loulou smiled. Normally by this time the young scallywag would have been dancing about, impatiently insisting they all 'Get Up and DO Something!' But not today. He was out for the count.

Loulou could see that Sylvester was half awake and half asleep, lying on her side in the early morning sunlight. Every now and then she stretched out her toes, as if getting ready to wake up, but then she would change her mind, her toes would relax, and she would be back in Dreamland.

This was a good thing in Loulou's opinion. The longer they slept, the more quickly his Deep Magic would dissolve all memory of their time-travelling adventures with King Richard. It would take many lifetimes for them to be ready to enjoy these memories in safety, the way that Loulou with all his centuries of wisdom could enjoy them. It was enough that they would remember how Winnie had protected Miss Chloe in the Castle and how the rest of them had swooped down on their carpet in the nick of time. And of course they would rejoice in knowing that Minnie the Mouser and The Hoodlum were gone forever.

Loulou now turned his attention to Hissie who was sleeping in such a tight ball that she looked like a fluffy grey pom-pom, making it hard to tell where she began

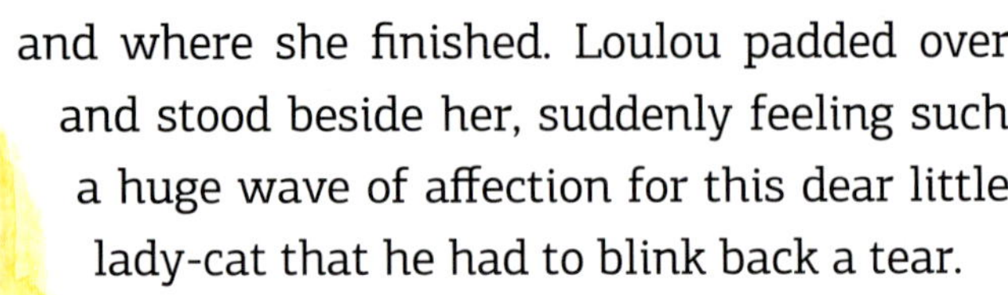

and where she finished. Loulou padded over and stood beside her, suddenly feeling such a huge wave of affection for this dear little lady-cat that he had to blink back a tear.

How many delicious meals had she made for everybody? How many times had she dropped whatever she was doing in order to give somebody (usually Winnie) a back rub or a kind word when it was needed? And how many times had she smiled and put on a brave face when inside she was quaking with fear? Because the truth was that Hissie was a worried little moggy, who jumped out of her skin at the slightest noise and who often had to go and sit in a quiet corner just to get through the day.

And since Winnie had come into their lives as a tiny kitten and now grown into a wild young man, she had become more worried than ever. She worried when he was at sea in case a storm blew up or he fell overboard. And she worried about Plug too, even though he was such an experienced old sea-cat. Whenever these two sailors were away on their boat she fretted, and then the night before their return she would get over-excited and not be able to sleep. And she even worried when Winnie was safely back at home in case he fell in with a bad crowd again.

And she worried that her mouse patties might not be crispy enough and that her catnip tea might not be strong enough...

And of course she worried about how she looked... Her fur was so fluffy that she would often say, 'I can't do a thing with it – I wish I could put my head in a paper bag...'

And it didn't matter how often they told her she was beautiful and that her catnip tea and special patties were the most delicious things in all the world, Hissie still worried. She worried about everything. It was just the way she was made.

And now, as he watched her lying there exhausted from the extra worries and excitements of the last couple of days, Loulou came to a decision. Hissie needed a holiday – a Proper Holiday – and she needed it right now.

So, as soon as he could rouse the others, he called a family meeting.

'Gather round,' he said. 'I've got an important announcement to make.'

And, even though they were still half asleep, they all pricked up their ears.

'To use a snuzzle expression,' Loulou said, 'I won't beat about the bush. I've decided we all deserve a holiday and so I've given permission for us to use the carpet purely for pleasure for the next few days, instead of using it only for Adventures and Emergencies. How does *that* sound?'

Not surprisingly, Winnie's voice was the first to be heard: 'Fantastic, Loulou! Can we go to that big Water Park and to one of those late-night football matches I've heard about? Oh, and I SO want to try kite surfing – and skateboarding *of course*...!'

Loulou was quick to respond. This was NOT what he had in mind for Hissie. 'I promise you, Winnie, that one day soon I *will* take you to those places but this holiday, this week, is going to be what snuzzles call R & R, which stands for Rest & Relaxation...'

He raised both his paw and his voice, as a shadow fell across Winnie's eager expression. '*Everybody* – including dashing young co-pilots – need a good rest from time to time to get their energy back, ready for their next Big Adventure. I've made a list of places we'll visit on our day trips but I'm going to keep it a surprise so each morning when we set off you won't know where we're going...'

His face then became more serious and he turned towards the fluffy grey pom-pom:

'Dear Hissie,' he began. 'None of us can thank you enough for the millions of delicious treats you have made for us, and for all our visitors, over the years. You have cared for all of us better than we deserve, so I want you to know that ALL our holiday meals will be provided so that you, too, will have a Proper Holiday. You won't have to lift a paw. You're going to snooze and nibble and enjoy the view and feel what it's like to be a queen. And by the end of the week you're going to feel WONDERFUL! How about a cheer for Hissie?!

And, as Hissie blushed and squirmed, Winnie and Sylvester joined Loulou in that famous song:

'For she's a jolly good moggy
For she's a jolly good moggy
For she's a jolly good moggy
And so say all of us!'

And, as the cheers died down, Loulou handed Hissie a small package wrapped in gold paper: 'This is your own special notebook, my dear, so that day by day you can write a few lines about your holiday. Then, in future years, you'll be able to read it and it will make you smile.'

Hissie was too moved to speak as she opened the package and found the most beautiful notebook imaginable, with a soft cover of mouse leather and pages made from the best quality parchment and with its own special quill pen and a bottle of cherry juice ink. She clutched it to her chest, smiled with eyes filled with tears, and trotted off to sit quietly by herself beside the lavender bush.

As soon as she had gone, Loulou put his arms around Winnie and Sylvester's shoulders, pulling them close, so he could whisper in their ears:

'Nothing – and I mean NOTHING – is to trouble Hissie over the next few days. If you get up to any hijinks, she *mustn't* find out. She's a nervous lady and we must all take extra care of her. This holiday is for all of us – but especially for her. *Do you both understand?'*

Winnie and Sylvester nodded their heads vigorously.

'Just one other thing,' Loulou added. 'Plug will be joining us whenever he can get a bit of free time, OK?'

'Hooray!' yelled Winnie. 'Hooray, hooray, hooray!' Everything was better when Plug was around. This would be a holiday to remember!

They set off early next morning and Loulou instructed the carpet to fly over the golden sands of Lady's Mile Beach. The sky was clear blue and the water glittered like turquoise beneath them, and Winnie was behaving so beautifully that Loulou allowed him to take the controls as they sailed gently along.

'This is a great honour, young man,' Loulou said. 'I'm counting on you to give us a smooth ride.'

'Yes, Captain!' said Winnie. 'You can depend on me!'

And he was as good as his word. Their flight was as smooth as silk – no tossing and bucking – and Hissie gazed out at the scenery in a trance, already beginning to feel her nervousness falling away as Loulou told them the story of the beach below:

'The reason it's called Lady's Mile is because many years ago an English soldier used to ride his favourite horse along these sands – and her name was Lady.'

They hovered along, 30 feet above the ground, completely invisible to the snuzzles enjoying the sand and sea below them. It reminded Winnie of their first test flight when they had flown over the Molos and he had snatched that chicken kebab and they had first met Plug. It made him smile a naughty smile but then he remembered he had promised to be a Very Good Boy today.

Loulou had decided that their main destination on this first day would be the famous Roman amphitheatre at Curium because he had visited it countless times over the 2000 years since it had been built and he knew all the nooks and crannies where they could spread out their picnic safely and undisturbed. So he took the controls from Winnie and steered them westwards.

Their first sight of this enormous circular outdoor theatre took their breath away. Carved from golden stone which shone with a dazzling light in the sunshine, it stood 20 rows high, going up, up, up like a massive curved staircase filling the whole landscape. Beyond it were fields, and then the same glistening Mediterranean Sea they had left behind at Lady's Mile Beach. Hissie was so overcome by the beauty all around that she clasped her paws in delight.

Loulou had never seen her so happy and that made him happy too.

'Aah,' he thought, smiling to himself. 'Everything's going to be *perfect*...!'

As they tucked into the delicious feast which the famous Limassol catering company 'Moggy Munchies and Lunchies' had magically spread out for them in a shady hideaway, Loulou did something he would later regret: he allowed Winnie to have a glass of catnip beer, thinking it would make the young chap drowsy so that he would have a nice long siesta.

Unfortunately, it didn't work out quite like that:

The beer had indeed made Winnie a little tipsy but, instead of making him nod off, it gave him what snuzzles call 'Dutch courage' so he felt cheeky and invincible and, without anyone noticing, he nipped off to explore right up at the very top of the theatre... And when he got there he felt so cheerful that he couldn't resist practising his latest craze – breakdancing... With the result that he tripped over his own feet and went tumbling down, down, down, bouncing over several layers of the hard stone seats like a rubber ball, before finally bumping to a stop.

Thank goodness, Hissie was so full of food that she was fast asleep and hadn't seen any of this. And thank goodness, too, that Sylvester *had* seen it. She grabbed Loulou's paw and the two of them rushed up to where the young scamp lay, covered in bruises and with a great big bumpy lump on his head and a cross-eyed expression on his face which would have been funny if they hadn't been so worried about him.

Loulou was greatly relieved to discover Winnie had no broken bones so they simply slathered him all over with the magical arnica ointment which Sylvester had grabbed out of Hissie's First Aid basket. Then they carried him carefully back down to the carpet (where Hissie was still sound asleep), put his co-pilot's cap back on his head so nobody could see the huge lumpy bump, and then poured another BIG glass of catnip beer down his throat to make sure he really did go to sleep for a very long time.

On the second day Loulou had arranged for them to go to the picturesque mountain village of Kakopetria, which is surrounded by orchards – apple trees, and pears and plums and apricots, peaches and cherries – making it the perfect place for a relaxing lunch. And, for Loulou, there were two added pleasures:

firstly, Plug would be joining them which always made him feel better; and secondly, he would be seeing his favourite cousin who lived and worked at a famous fish restaurant there. This cousin was half Scottish on his mother's side and was called Mr MacFurrson and he had assured Loulou that he would prepare a magnificent riverside banquet for them.

As the carpet travelled slowly over the pretty countryside, they could hear the splashing of the cool River Klarios below, and they filled up their lungs with fresh mountain air. And when the carpet finally came to rest under an overhanging tree on the riverbank, they could see that Mr MacFurrson had done them proud. Laid out were six very posh china dishes containing freshly cooked trout, oozing with butter, plus several saucers of catnip cream for pudding.

'No wonder Mr MacFurrson is so fat!' Winnie whispered to Sylvester. 'If I ate this every day I'd be fat too!'

'Shhh!' Sylvester chuckled, pretending to be cross. 'Just because you bumped your head yesterday doesn't mean you can be rude. *All* chefs in expensive restaurants have round tummies. It's the law...'

Loulou's cousin was indeed a very round gentleman and, like Loulou, he was all black. And as well as being twice as plump, he had unusual folded-down ears which Winnie thought was because he had to wear a chef's hat all the time but was actually because his mother had been a special kind of moggy known as a 'Scottish Fold' and all of them have folded-down ears.

But the main thing about Mr MacFurrson was that he was the kindest most generous moggy imaginable, with twinkling eyes and a loud rumbling laugh. 'Tuck in, tuck in everybody!' he said. 'There's plenty more if you want it!'

They accepted his invitation gratefully and soon had butter trickling down their chins. And, once they had eaten their fill, Plug kept Hissie company as she sat on a flat stone and dangled her toes in the clear water, and he explained to her that the field mice here were famously tasty and he caught four large specimens for her to take home to her larder. Loulou spent an hour catching up on all the news with his cousin; and Sylvester and Winnie sneaked around the corner for a dip, taking care to stay out of sight of Hissie because they knew she would worry about them going into the water with full tummies.

Promptly at half past three, Loulou clapped his paws and they all piled back on to the carpet. He was so relieved that there had been no further mishaps and that Hissie hadn't noticed that Winnie was still a bit dizzy and unsteady on his feet, that he had decided to round off the second day of their holiday with a visit to the village of Lania.

'It will be perfect for Hissie,' he explained to Plug. 'It's a peaceful place with little cobbled lanes where lots of snuzzle artists live and paint beautiful paintings. It's very pretty and everywhere there are old houses with colourful gardens and hanging baskets full of flowers and herbs. Hissie will love it!'

And he was right. As the carpet sailed merrily along, Hissie was so enchanted that she didn't know which way to look. In every direction there were so many interesting things: donkeys and windy lanes and colourful pot plants and deliciously scented herbs.

'Oh, Loulou,' she said. 'Do you think we could gather some of those herbs to take home to Malekidi Street to go with those lovely fresh field mice?'

'Yes, please, *do* let's get off and explore...!' whined Winnie, who had regained his energy since eating all that fish. 'Oh, *do* let's...!'

Loulou had to think fast. He didn't want to spoil the fun but nor did he want to take any risks with Winnie, not after yesterday's close shave.

'I've got a better idea,' he said. 'Why doesn't Mr Plug take Hissie down that little path to gather some herbs, and we can continue on a bit further because there's something even *more* interesting over there...'

Everyone decided this was a good plan and agreed to meet up again in an hour's time. That would give everyone time to enjoy themselves and, most importantly, it would keep Winnie out of Hissie's way.

As soon as they had dropped off Hissie and Plug, Loulou instructed the carpet to hover over one particular courtyard where a snuzzle artist had his easel all set up along with his table of brushes and paints, and all the paraphernalia which artists gather around them. Loulou and Sylvester

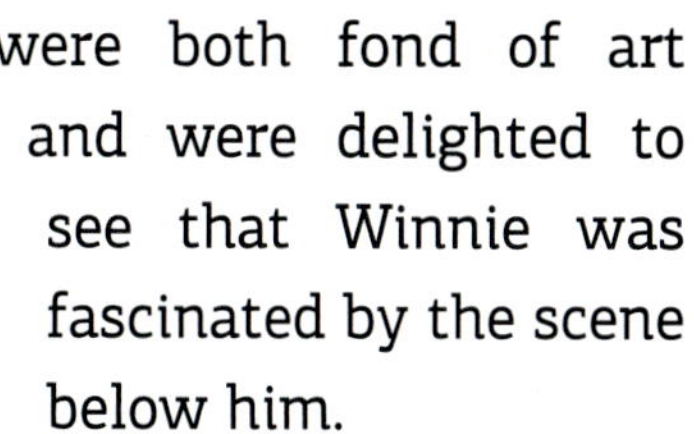

were both fond of art and were delighted to see that Winnie was fascinated by the scene below him.

Sitting on a chair beside a small fountain was a tall, stately-looking lady, who was keeping very still as the artist considered her carefully for the portrait he was painting.

Just above the lady's chair was a hanging basket filled with trailing nasturtiums and before long all three moggies were mesmerised by the soothing scene of the flowers and the fountain and the tall lady and the artist with his palette. But then it suddenly struck Winnie how nice it would be to give Hissie a gift. He could see that he would *just* be able to reach the nasturtiums in the hanging basket, while the artist was concentrating hard on a particularly difficult part of his painting. What could be nicer to give to your favourite auntie than a bunch of flowers?

And so it was that, as the carpet hovered silently above the peaceful scene, Winnie shot out his paw, swiped at the nasturtiums – and lost his balance... He hadn't taken into account that only yesterday he'd had a big bang on his head and was in no fit state to judge distances.

In two seconds flat the tranquil courtyard was a scene of pandemonium:

The lady screamed at the sight of a screeching moggy flying through the air, trailing nasturtiums from all four feet. She leapt up and rushed towards the house, tripping over in her hurry and landing in the fountain. The artist jumped sideways to avoid Winnie, bringing his easel crashing to the ground and sending pots and tubes of paint flying in all directions. The portrait landed face up on a little grassy patch and Winnie came down, splat, on top of it so that he was immediately covered in wet paint...

Instantly the carpet swooped down to scoop him up and, without a backward glance at the chaos behind them, they zoomed off to a quiet corner where Sylvester did her best to scrub Winnie's coat clean – without much success.

And Loulou sighed and wiped his forehead and thanked his lucky stars that all this time Hissie had been well away from the action, in the company of Plug, and he thought very hard about how he would explain Winnie's colourful coat to her...

Early next morning Loulou had a shock. As he checked his reflection in the window pane, he spotted a single white hair amongst the pure black fur of his handsome face.

Goodness me, he thought, these past couple of days of trying to keep Winnie's mishaps from Hissie have aged me! I must make sure things run more smoothly from now on. And he plucked out the white hair and pulled himself together.

'All right, everybody,' he said as soon as Plug had arrived and they had all piled on to the carpet. 'Today is going to be different. We're going to stay up in the air, all day long, no landing at all. Now watch this...!'

And they all gasped as the carpet rose into the air, growing massively in size as it did so, until, by the time they were hovering over the rooftop of Number 9 Malekidi Street, it was the size of a football pitch. They were all sitting right in the very middle of it and couldn't see to the edge.

'Over in that corner,' Loulou said, pointing to his left, 'I've set up a magical ladies' drawing room, just like we've seen in those Victorian serials which Katie Snuzzle watches on DVD in winter. This is so that Hissie and Sylvester can do ladylike things like reading books and playing games and trying on hats – or anything else they want. It's all been magicked into place with velvet sofas and plump cushions – and a leather armchair which will make a perfect scratching post.'

Then, as soon as Plug had escorted the ladies to their special room, Loulou turned to Winnie:

'Now, young man,' he said. 'I've arranged for Hissie to have an extra-quiet day with Sylvester, far away from you, which means that for this one day you can be as lively and bouncy as you want – just as long as you promise you'll be back on your best behaviour tomorrow, with no more loony escapades...'

'Yes, Loulou, of course, of course, of course...!'

And he bounded all the way over to the far side of the carpet and Loulou directed the carpet to fly northwards over the old deserted International Airport of Nicosia.

This was a strange place indeed and Winnie was spellbound as Loulou brought the carpet as low as he dared. Because of a big snuzzle argument years ago (in 1974) this airport has not been used from that day to this and, down there on the ground, Winnie could see old rusting aeroplanes sitting on crumbling runways, full of cracks and overgrown with weeds. The whole place was deserted – just like a ghost town – and there was the old Departures Building with broken windows and peeling paint and faded advertisements on the walls. And, through the broken windows, Winnie could see the rows of chairs where the passengers used to wait for their aeroplanes to be ready, only now there were no snuzzles at all, just piles of dead leaves and thick dust and birds swooping around.

To a young daredevil it was irresistible! Winnie leapt off the carpet, like a divebombing aeroplane, and darted in through a broken window, calling out as he did so, 'It's all right, Loulou, I promise I'm just going to have a peek, I'll be back in five minutes, I won't do anything to upset Hissie, honest...'

as the size of a football pitch

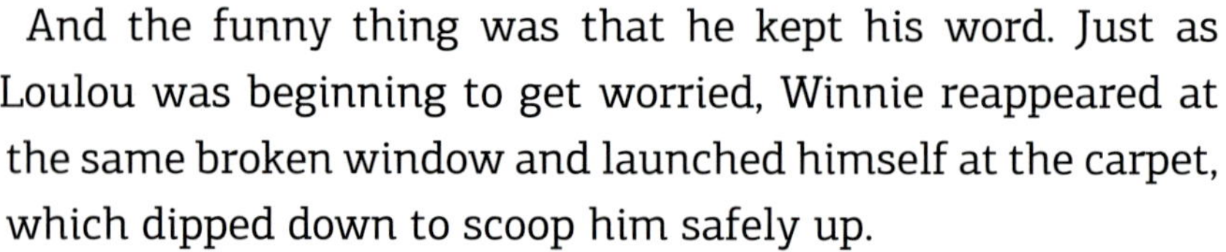

And the funny thing was that he kept his word. Just as Loulou was beginning to get worried, Winnie reappeared at the same broken window and launched himself at the carpet, which dipped down to scoop him safely up.

'Oh, Loulou, that was fantastic!' he said breathlessly. 'And it *was* fair. After all, I'm a real proper co-pilot, you couldn't expect me not to look around a deserted, spooky, dusty, GORGEOUS old airport, *could you*? And now I'm going to bounce up and down and over and over until all the dust has gone and nobody else will ever know I haven't been here with you the whole time...'

Loulou nodded his head in agreement. 'You're quite right, it's just the sort of place you *should* explore. And one day soon you and I will go off on our own on the carpet – maybe with Plug – and we'll spend a WHOLE DAY there!'

At these thrilling words, Winnie's somersaults and tumbles became so much more vigorous that all the dust had been beaten out of his coat in 10 seconds flat. And Loulou magicked up a skateboarding rink and a bouncy castle for him and said, 'Lunch is in one hour and then all this lot will disappear so make the most of it!'

And Winnie bounced and skated and dived and tumbled to his heart's content and no one would have guessed he had ever had a bump on the head. He felt wonderful.

As lunchtime approached, Loulou decided it was time to introduce Winnie to what he had hoped would be the biggest and most exciting surprise of the day.

They were flying over the central plain of Cyprus known as the Mesaoria, and Loulou pointed out to Winnie the strangely shaped hills and hummocks beneath them:

'Do you see those grassy mounds down there?' he asked.

'Yep,' replied Winnie in a rather bored voice, since he had bounced all the excitement out of himself.

'What do you think they are?'

'A load of old hills, of course.'

'Aah, but they're *not* just boring old hills,' said Loulou. 'In fact, I'm going to call the others over so they can see them too...'

'Whatever...' said Winnie, sounding even less impressed. 'I'm hungry...'

Once Hissie, Sylvester and Plug had joined them, Loulou pointed downwards again:

'Those aren't hills! They're sleeping dragons and they rise up when – and ONLY when – the Lords of the Earth and Sky call them...'

'And how often does *that* happen?' Winnie asked, with a yawn. Fairy stories were just for kids...

'About once in a million years – when there's a REAL problem or when the planet is in REAL trouble...'

'Hrrrrmph…' snorted Winnie. 'So *I'm* not likely to see one wake up then…' he mumbled. 'I bet it's just a silly old story anyway… What's for lunch?'

Loulou sighed. Honestly, sometimes he didn't understand Winnie at all. How could he be so excited about a dusty old airport and then not the least bit thrilled at the idea of a grassy hill turning out to be a sleeping dragon? The younger generation were a mystery even to a wise old moggy like Loulou.

But Winnie would have kicked himself if he had seen what happened next…

They had all eaten another magnificent lunch provided by the chef at Moggy Munchies and Lunchies. Plug had taken the ladies aside to teach them a gentle hornpipe dance before they settled down for their siesta, and Winnie was lying on his back, looking at the sky and feeling very snoozy after all his earlier exertions. So it was only Loulou, quietly drinking his peppermint tea and gazing over the landscape, who clearly saw one of the grassy mounds take a great heaving breath, up and down, and swish its grassy tail from side to side, before blowing a huge smoke ring up into the sky and then sinking down into complete stillness once more. Loulou smiled and looked lovingly over to where Winnie was now fast asleep, having missed what could have been the most exciting event of his life.

Hissie's Diary, Wednesday
Sylvester and I had a lovely time in our Magic Parlour. I read an interesting book by a wise moggy called Deecat Chapra. I won three times at Ludo but Sylvester got her own back by beating me at snakes and ladders. Winnie, too, had a very quiet day, bless his little cotton socks…

Next day, everyone was amazed to see that Loulou had ordered enough lunch for at least 100 moggies!

'Goodness me!' Hissie exclaimed, her eyes like saucers. 'I know you want me to put on some weight, Loulou, but isn't this going a little far?!'

Loulou chuckled and, as they floated up into the blue sky, he explained why he had ordered so many provisions:

'I know how much **Hissie** enjoys helping those less fortunate than herself,' he said. 'So today we're going to give a feast to some very special moggies who are having a lean time of it at the moment. And all this lovely food also

159

contains magical medicine to heal their ailments so, not only will they get a nourishing meal, but when they wake up after their next long sleep they'll feel as good as new – and they won't know how or why! It will be our secret!'

'What a wonderful idea! But who *are* these special moggies?' Hissie asked.

'They live at the Monastery of St Nicholas of the Cats,' Loulou replied. 'Does everybody know the story?'

Sylvester and Hissie nodded their heads but Winnie looked puzzled. 'I don't think so… And yet I seem to have a funny kind of memory about it. It's very strange…'

'Well,' said Loulou, 'the story goes like this: More than 1500 years ago, our beloved island was full of poisonous snakes. It was so bad that almost all the snuzzles ran away, leaving the island pretty much deserted – until a clever lady called Helena brought a whole shipload of fearless moggies from Egypt and Palestine to kill the snakes and make the place safe again for snuzzles. And her plan worked – of course,' said Loulou. 'And everyone was so grateful that they built a monastery there and made a law that the monks who lived there must care for 100 moggies and feed them twice a day.'

'Hear hear!' said Hissie and Sylvester. And Winnie added, 'I should think so, too!'

'Unfortunately,' Loulou continued, 'the monastery has been through some tough times over the years (all because of silly snuzzle battles, of course) but now, once again, there are lots of moggies living there – and almost no snakes! But, sadly, there isn't enough money to feed them properly, so that's why we're taking our special magic food-medicine.'

And so it was that a couple of hours later the Malekidi Moggies found themselves surrounded by hordes of rather dilapidated but delighted moggies of every shape and size and colour, tucking into a magical feast. They were so grateful that some were dancing for joy while others were so overcome that they had tears rolling down their cheeks. But they were happy tears and so Hissie was happy too – especially since she knew that all their aches and pains and diseases would also soon be gone.

And it was such a merry scene that nobody noticed that Winnie had disappeared...

He couldn't explain it. He had seemed to hear a magical kind of music in his head and it led him round the corner and up a path to a small stony place which was completely deserted. At least it *looked* deserted...

But then, all of a sudden, Winnie got a funny feeling in his spine and he knew that it wasn't deserted at all and he spun round to find himself staring straight into the eyes of an ugly fat old snake. 'But Loulou said there wouldn't be any snakes!' he said to himself, starting to tremble. 'Especially not *this* kind of snake!' Because Winnie had recognised this one as a blunt-nosed viper, the ugliest and deadliest snake in Cyprus...

But before he had time to think, he was caught up in a battle royal. Winnie bared his teeth and his ears went back and his hair puffed up all around him as he dodged this way and that, trying to avoid the reptile's poisonous

fangs. He slashed at the beast with his long claws, desperately trying to get a strike that would frighten him away. But it was useless. Even though the snake was fat, it was incredibly fast, doubling back on itself at breakneck speed, and Winnie didn't dare turn his back and try to run away, but nor could he see a way of getting out of this situation alive.

Until, all of a sudden, that strange mystical music in his head started up again and he remembered the old Indian cat, Mog Dahl, and what he had told him he must do in such a situation. Winnie could have sworn he actually *heard* that old moggy whispering in his ear: 'Stare into his eyes, Winnie, just stare and stare into his snaky eyes… You'll be OK… Stand still and stare… TRUST ME!'

So that's exactly what Winnie did and, would you believe it, as soon as he stared into that viper's eyes, not only did the snake stop fighting and spitting and hissing but it got a gooey look on its face and said, 'Wait a minute! I *know* you, don't I?!'

'And I know you, too!' Winnie replied, with a giggle.

'Do you remember that first battle we had?' the snake said, 'all those hundreds of years ago when that woman brought you moggies into Cyprus to give us snakes a hard time?!'

'Yes!' said Winnie. 'And you and I decided not to be stupid so instead of trying to kill each other, we ran off and went our separate ways unharmed!'

'That's it!' And the snake grinned and sang a line from a famous snuzzle song: "All we are saying is give peace a chance!" And the two of them laughed and laughed until they cried.

It wasn't often that Loulou was beside himself with excitement. He was such a dignified gentleman that nothing really fazed him. But he was so thrilled by the treat he had planned for the fifth day of Hissie's holiday that he could hardly contain himself.

'Where are we *going*?!' Winnie kept asking every five minutes. 'And why are we all dressed up?'

Because, instead of having a day trip, Loulou had informed the others, including Plug, that they must have lots of extra sleep during the day and then spend at least three hours making themselves especially smart for the evening's surprise.

It was only when they were finally gathered on the carpet an hour after sunset that Loulou explained:

'We're only going down the road a little way but, in another way, we're going into a different world... We're going to the THEATRE! – a proper snuzzle THEATRE! And the way we're going to get inside is extra specially magical... '

And so it was.

The carpet lifted up into the night sky and travelled along Malekidi Street until it was hovering outside the famous Rialto Theatre, where lots of smartly dressed snuzzles were chattering excitedly and queueing up to go inside.

'ONE NIGHT ONLY!' said the big poster outside. 'INTERNATIONAL CAST FOR THE GREATEST MUSICAL OF ALL TIME: **CATS!**'

'Yes,' beamed Loulou as he saw his friends' eyebrows all shoot up. 'A theatrical extravaganza about the most important subject of all – moggies! Moggies, moggies, moggies!'

And they all cheered and Winnie did a handstand so that his co-pilot's cap flew off and Plug just managed to catch it before it disappeared over the edge of the carpet.

'Now, for the next two minutes, you need to lie down very still, in a neat row,' Loulou instructed. They all obeyed and the carpet rolled itself over and over around them until it was a long thin tube. Remember that as long as they were on the carpet they were completely invisible so now, as the last of the snuzzles took their seats, the long tube of carpet with the moggies safely tucked up inside simply zoomed in through the theatre door, unnoticed by anyone. Easy peasy!

And as soon as it was inside the theatre, it unrolled itself again until it was the size of two large dining room tables, hovering two feet above the snuzzles' heads in the very best seats near the front. The Malekidi Moggies had the best view in the whole theatre, and yet nobody could see them. What a perfect arrangement!

They stretched out comfortably, feeling very grand and excited, and helped themselves to the glasses of pink catnip champagne which Loulou had magicked for

them, along with some cheesy biscuits and mouse crisps.

To see all those snuzzles dressed up as moggies, singing and dancing on the stage, was an experience they would talk about for the rest of their lives. Hissie thought her little heart would burst with happiness; and Plug hummed along to all the tunes because he knew them already; and Winnie and Sylvester made a Dare with each other that *somehow* they would join in the chorus line at the back; and Loulou smiled and beamed as he shared in the happiness of his little family.

But there was some drama off stage as well as on it...

In the interval, the carpet rolled itself up into a tube again and took the Malekidi Moggies a little way down the road where they could get off and stretch their legs without being seen. And, as Hissie was powdering her nose, a tall elegant gentleman cat approached her, bowed, and offered her a glass of geranium wine, which she accepted with a blushing smile. He was full of compliments about her beautiful silvery grey fur and offered her his calling card: 'Perhaps we could meet again one evening?' he purred. 'We could get to know each other a little better over dinner or perhaps you would like to go for a walk after the show...?'

At that point the bell sounded, letting everyone know it was time to go back into the theatre for the second half of the performance and, in all the bustle, Hissie became separated from her charming admirer. At the same time, Plug was whispering urgently to Loulou, 'Do you know who that is?' he asked, pointing at the smooth gent. 'It's Red Rick who works for Fur Fingers – that underworld gang... And I happen to know that they're planning to make a luxurious fur muff for the spoilt daughter of a Russian billionaire. Our beloved Hissie is falling under his spell and it's her fluffy coat he's after... I'm going to sort this out...' And before Loulou could speak, Plug had rolled up his sleeves and disappeared.

The next two minutes were ones that Red Rick would never forget. Scarcely had he put away his silver card case, than he found himself dragged into a dark alley by a tough-looking old sea-cat in a dinner jacket and a velvet eyepatch.

'If you lay a single paw on Miss Hissie,' Plug snarled ferociously, 'you're dead meat... Understand?' And before the shocked cad could reply, he found himself on the receiving end of the biggest knockout punch he had ever experienced. It was such a corker that, before he passed out, he couldn't help thinking what a useful member of his gang this stranger would have been and he vowed to keep out of his way in future.

Brushing the dust off his jacket and smoothing his ruffled whiskers, Plug was just in time to dive into the tube of the carpet as it zoomed back inside the theatre. He gave the thumbs-up sign to Loulou, who heaved a huge sigh of relief, and they all settled down to enjoy the second act – and another glass of catnip champagne.'

Hmmm… Sometimes it's better not to know what is right around the corner…

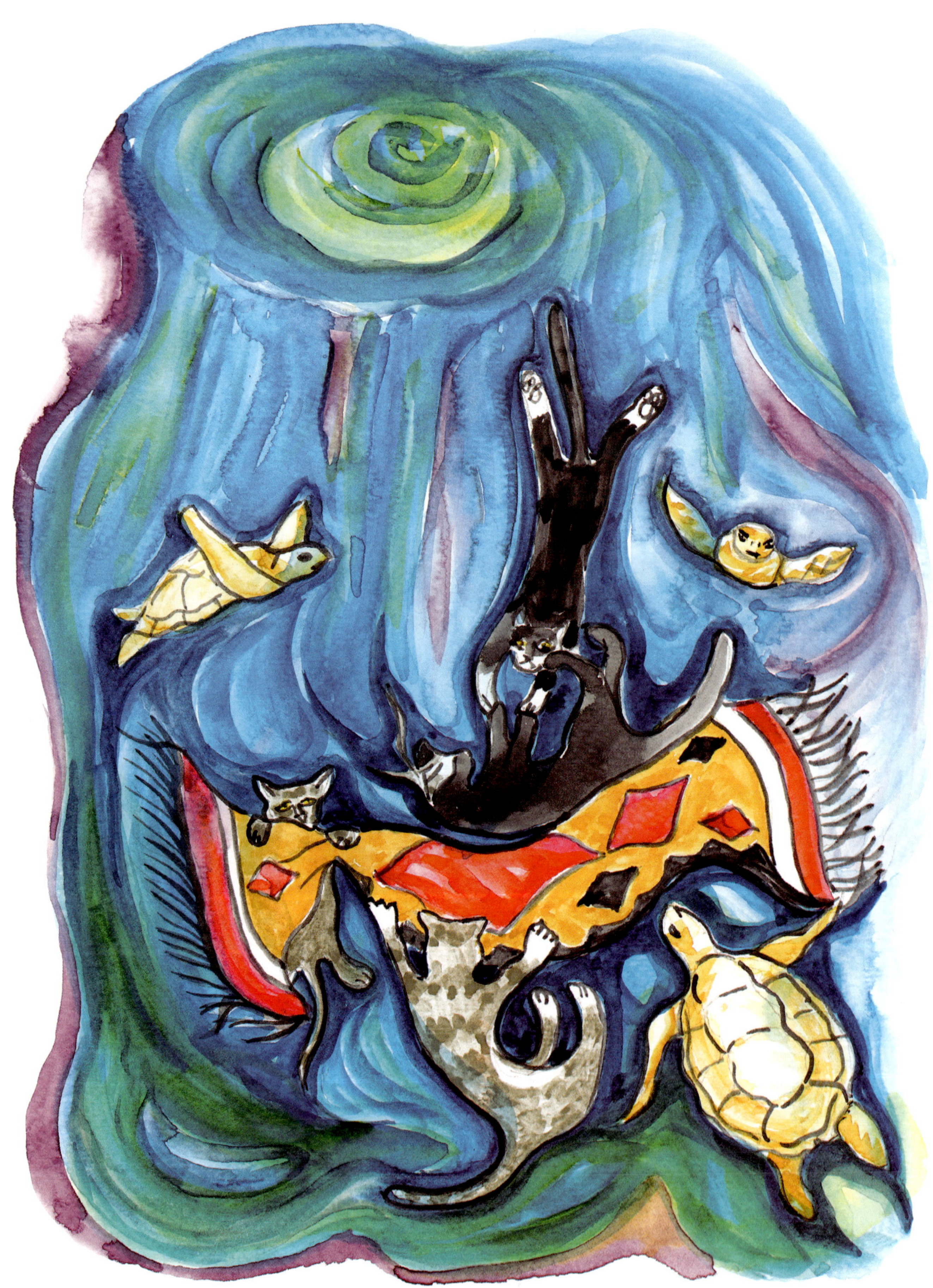

8

CAT-ASTROPHE!

'Chop chop!' said Loulou, tapping Winnie on the bum. 'Only five minutes till take-off and I need my trusty co-pilot by my side!' Then he turned and called across to Hissie and Sylvester, who were gazing at their reflections in the window pane, making sure that their whiskers were neat and tidy, their noses pink and shiny: 'Come along ladies, all aboard!'

It was 8.30 the next morning – the last day of their first ever holiday – and the sun was shining out of a clear blue Limassol sky.

They piled on to the carpet, which was stretched out in the garden, already stacked with its daily supply of picnic baskets and bottles of interesting things to drink.

'Now, listen very carefully,' Loulou said as they settled down, their heads and hearts bursting with eager anticipation.

'First of all, we are sitting inside a Breathing Bubble! You can't see it but it's all around us and it's extremely important because today we're going to fly right up, high above the clouds to 40,000 feet, and the air is so thin up there that we need our Breathing Bubble so that we can breathe properly, just like we do when we're on the ground.'

Loulou looked at the three faces in front of him. Needless to say, Winnie was twitching with excitement. 'Wowy-zowy!' he gasped, and 'Amazing!' and '40,000 feet! – *Too Much!*' Sylvester looked wide-eyed and thrilled but Loulou could tell that little

Hissie was having an attack of the collywobbles. 'Now, don't worry, my dear!' he said kindly. 'There's nothing more relaxing than flying high above the Earth. It's so *quiet* up there! Trust me, you'll *love* it. In fact, I especially chose this particular outing for our last day-trip because it will be the most spectacular but also the most tranquil. So we can *all* be happy!'

Hissie smiled and let herself relax. Of course there was nothing to worry about, she thought. Look how perfect the previous five days had been. This one would be even better. Admittedly, she did rather wish that Plug could have been with them but he had promised Yiannos, Panos and Phanos that he would do an extra day's work on the boat and he didn't like going back on his word.

So it was just the four Malekidi Moggies who sailed up into the clear blue sky, sipping their early morning catnip tea from the thermos flask, and breathing as comfortably as ever inside Loulou's magic Breathing Bubble.

Up and up they floated, leaving the garden and the whole of Malekidi Street and then the whole of Limassol far, far below them. Winnie had brought along his latest craze: a bamboo flute which he had found in a rubbish bin. He hoped that, if he practised enough, he would be able to join the Malekidi Monsters at The Cat's Whiskers and he dreamed of performing solos which would make all those nice young girl-cats go weak at the knees.

He was tootling happily away as the carpet glided over a place with the complicated name of Shillourokambos and Loulou announced that he had a funny story to tell them about it:

'It was down there,' he said, pointing thousands of feet below them, 'that some snuzzle scientists discovered the very first signs of moggies and snuzzles living together. They found the remains of a snuzzle and a moggy curled up together and they were EIGHT THOUSAND years old!'

Winnie had put down his flute and whistled through his teeth. '8,000 years, Loulou! *Really*?!'

'Yes!' Loulou said with a grin. 'But here's the funny part: the scientists said that it was 8,000 years since snuzzles first domesticated cats! Yes! They honestly believe that *they* domesticated *us* when we all know that it was the other way around! Honestly, they're such hopelessly lovable creatures! How would they ever cope without us?!'

And as the carpet continued to soar higher and higher, the Malekidi Moggies rolled about in fits of the giggles on its shiny silken surface.

Laughter and a wonderful view and the company of dear friends. What could possibly go wrong?

Quite a lot, as it turned out...

A mere half an hour later, as they were tucking into their elevenses and the carpet had finally reached what pilots call its Cruising Altitude, something caught Loulou's attention and everything changed...

'What's going on over there?' he said anxiously, pointing to a large jet aeroplane just 50 yards away. 'Something's not right...'

Winnie, Hissie and Sylvester turned to look in the direction Loulou was pointing and, yes, they could all see that something was indeed very, very wrong.

In the couple of hours since they had left the ground, they had passed several aircraft – passenger jets like this one, bringing holidaymakers and business people to Cyprus; and noisy military jets whizzing about on exercises; and lots of little private planes and helicopters buzzing about like insects. And now, up here at 40,000 feet, there were all sorts of enormous planes, cruising their way between cities as far apart as Sydney and Paris, or Johannesburg and London. All the jets they had seen so far had looked sleek and beautiful, shining in the bright sunlight, moving as gracefully across the sky as an ocean liner on a calm sea. But not this one!

It was as if its pilots didn't know what they were doing. The plane was going up and down and this way and that, all over the place like a crazy thing. By now the carpet was only 20 yards away from it and the Malekidi Moggies could clearly see the pilot in his smart blue uniform and his co-pilot with a cap just like Winnie's. But who was *that*?! There was a third man in the cockpit, waving something about and shouting angrily at the two pilots. No wonder they weren't concentrating on keeping the plane steady!

'Oh my goodness!' exclaimed Loulou, as the truth dawned on him. 'This is what snuzzles call a hijacking! That wild-looking fellow is brandishing a gun! He must be demanding that they fly the plane somewhere else – I'm not surprised the pilots look so terrified!'

They certainly did! The moggies were close enough now to see that both men were as white as sheets while the third man, who was wearing dark sunglasses and a baseball cap, was so angry that his face was almost purple.

'We've got to *do* something!' Loulou said with a great sense of urgency. 'Listen, I'm going to cause a distraction. Now, don't you worry! It will only take me half a minute and then it will be up to the pilots to save their plane and their passengers...'

And before any of them could speak, Loulou had muttered a secret incantation and had begun to grow in size before their very eyes. In a matter of seconds, he had expanded and expanded to the size of an enormous black panther, and his eyes were blazing with green fire, and sparks were flashing from his whiskers and he pulled his lips back in a terrifying snarl to reveal a pair of razor-sharp fangs.

The sight was so awe-inspiring that Winnie, Hissie and Sylvester were stunned into silence and didn't even have time to be afraid.

Then they all gasped in unison as Loulou brought the carpet right up close to the side window of the plane's cockpit and, with one enormous leap, hurled himself on to the nose of the speeding aircraft.

He didn't have a moment to lose. Now that he was off the carpet, he was no longer inside the protective Breathing Bubble. Everything depended on the next 10 seconds...

He thumped his massive paw against the glass of the windscreen so that the men inside turned to look at him. And all three of their faces showed stunned disbelief and their eyes came out on stalks – because what they saw, at 40,000 feet above the Earth, was the biggest, most ferocious looking wild cat they could ever have imagined. It was snarling and banging on the glass, and spitting and hissing and sending out showers of sparky green flames which looked as if they might engulf the whole plane.

On the carpet, Winnie had both his front paws stuffed inside his mouth; Hissie had her eyes tight shut and was muttering 'I'm a warrior, not a worrier' over and over;

and Sylvester had forgotten how to breathe. The seconds were ticking away but it also seemed as if Time were standing still.

And then, all of a sudden, there was a flash of movement from inside the cockpit. The co-pilot had snatched his opportunity and done a fantastic karate chop on the hijacker who had been momentarily distracted by the crazy vision outside the window. And as the co-pilot whacked the hijacker in the guts and then on the back of his neck, the captain grabbed the gun and leapt on top of the purple-faced man, and the co-pilot took over the controls once again.

By this time, all the air in Loulou's lungs was completely used up and he was desperate to take another breath. Seeing that his plan had worked, he felt a huge surge of relief and hurled himself back on to the carpet. At least he *almost* hurled himself back on to the carpet...

Because, for a split second, he had forgotten just how enormous he now was and so he misjudged his jump by a few inches and would have plummeted to the ground and certain death if the carpet had not lunged sideways underneath him to break his fall.

Phew, that was close...!

But, even though the worst catastrophe had not happened, things were far from OK because Loulou had hit his head with great force on the side of the plane. All he heard was an almighty *Crack* and then everything went black.

For the passengers and crew of the plane, the most dangerous part of the drama was over but for the Malekidi Moggies the nightmare had just begun...

'Loulou! Oh, Loulou!' cried Hissie the instant he landed with a dreadful thud in the middle of the carpet. 'Oh, Loulou, please *say* something!'

But they could all see that it would be a long time before their beloved friend and mentor spoke again – if he *ever* spoke again... The gash on the side of his head was bleeding and there was an ugly purple bruise over his left eye and it was swelling up in a scary sort of way. And he was completely still – so still that Winnie felt his blood freeze in his veins as he thought the dreadful, unthinkable thought: what if Loulou *never* woke up? What if he died? And, *oh no!* What if he was dead already?

Hissie and Sylvester had dragged over the First Aid basket and were gently and tearfully bathing Loulou's wound with witch hazel lotion before dabbing his bruises with arnica ointment and carefully wrapping a white bandage around his poor battered head.

Trembling with fear, Sylvester put her paw on his chest and then under his nose:

'There is a very faint pulse,' she said, trying to swallow back her tears. 'And I can *just* feel the breath going in and out of his nose but, oh my goodness, he is very weak. He saved those snuzzles in their plane,' she said. 'Oh, I couldn't *bear* it if we lost him...' And she put her arm around Hissie's shoulder and they both wept hot silent tears and prayed as hard as they could for their dearest friend.

But just a few seconds later they were snapped out of their misery by two things: first, the carpet started vibrating and shaking in the most alarming manner; and, second, Winnie's voice, sounding very grown-up all of a sudden, cut through the air like a knife:

'My dear Auntie Hissie and Auntie Sylvester, there is something you must understand. *The carpet is completely out of control.* It will only respond to Loulou's commands – no one else's. When we flew over Lady's Mile Beach the other day, Loulou officially handed the controls to me and so the carpet obeyed *my* commands. But he didn't do that today. There was no time. He just leapt off the carpet to do what he had to do to save the plane and then...'

His voice trailed off and he found himself gulping for air as he tried to keep his nerve and say what had to be said: 'I'm sure the carpet is now reacting to all the chaos in Loulou's brain, that's why it's diving all over the place. We have to face the facts: we're stuck up here on an out-of-control carpet and, if we're going to save our own lives and also dear Loulou's life, we must keep our heads and Think Straight! We can't cry and get scared! We *mustn't!* Our lives depend on it! The carpet is already beginning to descend. I'm sorry but... but... we're probably going to crash...'

'But what can we *do*?' wailed Hissie and Sylvester in unison. 'If the carpet won't take orders from you, what can we *do*?'

'We need to keep Loulou as calm and comfortable as possible,' Winnie replied. 'If we can soothe his brain and keep him warm and feeling safe, then maybe the carpet itself will calm down a bit. We must accept that we're going to have a very bumpy landing but the good thing is that we've got some time because we're starting from so very high up...'

And as the three of them tried with all their might to concentrate on keeping Loulou calm and warm, they were all thinking the same thing: If only Plug were here! Things never looked so bleak or so black when Plug was around. He had a comforting presence that made everything seem OK, even in the middle of a great big storm at sea. But he wasn't around, was he? He was miles away, down there somewhere on The Courageous Sea-Cat, completely unaware of their plight.

Hissie gently stroked Loulou's brow, still reminding herself that she must be a warrior, not a worrier. And Winnie tried to imagine himself as the superhero, Mick the Monster Mog, who saved the planet from disaster every single week in the pages of 'Ker-Zow! The Comic for Cool Cats'. And Sylvester tucked a blanket all around Loulou's body to keep him snug and then she tried to think of ways she could help the others with their swimming skills when they landed, crash bang wallop, in the water.

And just for a moment she thought, 'Oh my goodness, what if we don't crash into the sea but on to dry land? We wouldn't have a chance...' But then she shut her eyes tight and made a supreme effort to push such a terrible thought from her mind by saying firmly and clearly:

'We *will* land in the sea. It will be scary and dangerous but we *will* survive! We *must* survive! The Malekidi Moggies Will Not Die!'

While Hissie and Sylvester did their best to soothe Loulou by singing to him and stroking him gently with their velvety paws, Winnie tried as hard as he could to communicate with the carpet. He kept touching the magic golden thread which Hissie had stitched into his co-pilot's cap but all that seemed to do was disturb Loulou because, after all, it had been put there so that Winnie could contact Loulou in an emergency, not so that he could give orders to the carpet.

'Surely there's *something* I can do!' he kept muttering to himself. But the harder he tried the more hopeless the situation seemed. 'What use is a co-pilot who can't take over in an emergency?' he asked himself. And then he added, 'I'm too *young* to die!'

But as the minutes ticked by, it became more and more clear that this was a real possibility. He could tell by the way the scene below was changing that they were losing height. He estimated they must now be at 20,000 feet, halfway down. 'That gives us about an hour...' he thought with a shiver.

He looked across at his beloved friends – one of them close to death and the other two doing everything they could to keep their own spirits up at the same time as using all their nursing skills to give Loulou the best possible chance of survival.

All the happy times they had shared – as well as all those times when he had been naughty and driving them nuts – flashed across Winnie's mind. He couldn't have wished for a better or kinder family. And they might never have the opportunity to laugh together again. He felt tears pricking his eyes and brushed them angrily away.

Loulou had always told him that they would never really be separated, even if one of them did die. And Mog Dahl had told him that all moggies jumped in and out of their bodies all the time, dying and being born, going and coming, sometimes as a tabby, sometimes a tortoiseshell, sometimes posh, sometimes riffraff, sometimes fat, sometimes thin, for hundreds and thousands of lifetimes. In fact, Loulou himself had told Winnie that dying and being reborn was just like walking from one room into another, nothing to worry about. Winnie trusted everything that Loulou and Mog Dahl told him but, now that they really were in mortal danger, he was finding it hard to keep believing.

As the carpet continued its descent, they all found it helped if they kept busy so they took it in turns to tend to Loulou and to drink endless cups of catnip tea to soothe their own frazzled nerves.

But no amount of tea could disguise the fact that they were getting closer and closer to the ground and, to make matters worse, the closer they got, the crazier the carpet became. Fortunately, it hadn't speeded up – they knew that if they plummeted into the ground at full pelt, they wouldn't stand a chance – but, even so, their slow, steady descent and the carpet's unpredictable behaviour was making them more frightened than ever.

A little earlier, the carpet had actually quietened down a bit as they had first started to soothe Loulou, but now it had started to dip and dive again with alarming violence so they had to hang on with their claws. It bucked and rose up and plunged down and flipped and slithered, and all the time the sea was getting closer and closer.

'Let's all be thankful for small mercies,' Sylvester said. 'I was worried we might crash on to the land and that would definitely have been the end of us. But it looks as if we're going to crash into the sea which means at least we've got a chance...'

Hissie's attempts to be a warrior, not a worrier were fading by now and all the stuffing had drained out of Winnie so that he was barely recognisable as the cool flute-playing dude of just two hours ago.

They were now all huddled together around Loulou, their arms draped about each other's shoulders in a loving group-hug as they watched the sea rising up to meet them.

'There will be an enormous crash and splash when we hit the water,' Sylvester explained. 'At the last moment, we must each take a very big breath in and then, when we find ourselves under the water, we mustn't panic. Trust me, if you hold your breath in your lungs and relax as best you can, you'll float back up to the surface and then I'll help you to swim for the shore. We'll have to leave the carpet behind but we'll be able to support Loulou, I'm *sure* we will...'

Actually, she wasn't nearly as sure as she sounded but she *did* know how to swim and she would do everything in her power to save her friends, including the unconscious Loulou.

'What's *that*?!' Winnie suddenly said, pointing directly below them. 'Oh no, Sylvester, it looks as if we're going to land on the *rocks*!'

Sure enough, there was no doubt about it. Even though they were well out to sea (which meant there would be a long swim back to the shore even if they did survive the crash), they would indeed have had a chance. But the patch of sea they were heading for just happened to be jam-packed with rocks which were clearly visible just under the surface of the water.

'So this is it, then,' they all thought. 'We're doomed. Of all the patches of sea we could be about to hit, it just happens to be the patch that is strewn with treacherous rocks!'

They hugged each other more tightly, shut their eyes, creased up their faces, and took an enormous breath in, at the same time as making sure that Loulou was as safely cushioned as they could manage...

And then...

SPLAT! SPLASH! CRASH!

The carpet hit the water with massive force and it felt as if Time had suddenly stopped as they braced themselves in readiness for the deadly rocks to smash them to pieces once and for all.

'Am I dead?' thought Winnie, as the world went all heavy and quiet and black around him.

And, 'Am I dead?' thought Hissie as the waters closed over her head and she felt herself being pressed down, down, down into the dark.

And, 'Am I dead?' thought Sylvester as she scrambled to keep a tight hold on Loulou, although she couldn't even feel her own paws.

And then they all realised that, No, they weren't dead, even though their lungs were bursting and they were terrified out of their wits by the thunderous silence of the sea as they continued to be pushed down into its cold and inky depths.

And then, still somehow clinging to the sodden, sinking carpet, they all asked themselves the same question:

'What happened to those rocks? We slammed right down on top of them and yet they aren't here...'

It was true. By now the carpet should have been slashed to ribbons by the rocks they had so clearly seen just beneath the surface of the water. They themselves should have been dashed to pieces. But apart from the fact that they were now under several feet of water and trying desperately to make their last tiny bit of air last a few more moments, they could tell that they had *not* crashed on to any rocks at all. Why? – and *how*?

'Never mind How and Why,' they each told themselves sternly. 'We've got a chance now! We haven't a clue what's happened but it's just possible that we can survive!'

Hissie and Winnie grabbed on to Sylvester's tail and they all hung on to Loulou as, in some strange inexplicable way, they felt the waterlogged carpet beginning to be gently raised up, up, up.

None of it made any sense to them but they were so stunned with relief as they began to sense the sunlight above them, that they didn't care whether it made any sense or not.

And then, just as they thought their lungs would explode, their heads burst through the surface of the water and they sprawled on the carpet, their chests heaving, their eyes stinging from the salt, their fur so wet and clinging to them so tightly that they truly did look like drowned rats.

With her last ounce of strength, Sylvester managed to crawl over to Loulou and press her head to his chest. To her relief she could tell that his heart was still beating, even though very weakly, and he was an even sorrier sight now that his jet black fur was sticking to his body and his bandages had been half washed away.

And now, as their heads gradually began to clear, they all

turned their attention to the mystery of the missing rocks. Because the rocks had not only disappeared but it had felt as if those very rocks had been *cushioning* the carpet as it crashed into the water – as if they were in fact not rocks at all but springy water mattresses or trampolines...

What on earth could have happened...? Maybe they *were* dead and this was some strange afterworld... Or maybe they had quite simply gone mad and weren't seeing or thinking straight.

But what was this! All of a sudden a round head bobbed up beside them and peeked over the edge of the carpet where they were all sprawled in their exhaustion.

'Are you all right?' came an anxious voice. 'We did our best!'

And to the amazement of Winnie, Hissie and Sylvester, they found themselves looking into the smiling eyes of none other than Myrtle Turtle!

'I promised I would repay you one day!' she said. 'You saved my life and now I've helped to save yours!'

'But... How... What on earth...?' spluttered the Malekidi Moggies.

'There are hundreds of us!' Myrtle said. 'The "rocks" you saw were us waiting for you! You've been rescued by the Turtle Armada! We all got into position and when our Admiral gave the command, we all sank down underneath you at just the right speed so that we could cushion your fall and keep the carpet – which was immediately very heavy from all the water – from sinking to the bottom of the sea, taking you all with it...'

She shuddered at the thought and so did the Malekidi Moggies.

'Do you mean,' Sylvester said, 'that when we looked down and saw rocks, we were actually seeing all you turtles just beneath the surface of the water?!'

'Yes!' said Myrtle. 'I'll explain it properly to you later – and you'll meet all my friends and relations – but now we must concentrate on getting you safely to the shore and it's a long long way...'

'Oh thank you, thank you, THANK YOU!' exclaimed the Malekidi Moggies. 'But how did you know we needed help in the first place?!'

By way of reply, Myrtle pointed her flipper to the sky: 'Look up there!'

Winnie, Hissie and Sylvester could hardly believe their eyes! Hovering 50 feet above their heads was a large fishing basket – a fishing basket suspended from the feet of a massive seagull – a seagull whom Winnie recognised immediately! It was Walter, the lookout gull from The Courageous Sea-Cat! And not only that but who should be in that fishing basket, with a telescope to his eye and the other paw waving at them, but Plug himself!

Myrtle was continuing to explain: 'Walter happened to spot you when you were having that scary encounter with the big jet aeroplane and he immediately flew back to the boat and told Plug, who sent Walter straight off to find *me* and then I contacted the Turtle High Command! Then Walter and Plug followed all your movements and kept reporting back so that we could all come together and position ourselves just right. This has been the most exciting – and scary – day of my life! Even more scary than the time *you* rescued *me!*'

'Ahoy there!' came Plug's comfortingly familiar voice as the basket descended. 'The turtles will have you heading safely towards the shore in a jiffy. It's a long way but the main thing is you're all safe!'

And immediately the Admiral gave the command to his massive armada to start hauling the carpet towards the shore, keeping it safely above the surface of the water as they did so.

Despite their exhaustion, the Malekidi Moggies felt themselves beginning to relax and their hearts to lift. They were going home! Myrtle and her friends were taking them home. They would get help for Loulou and all would be well.

Unfortunately, it was not to be quite that easy...

The poor turtles had used up every ounce of energy in the initial rescue. Their plan had worked perfectly but they had not bargained for the fact that they were now trying to swim against the wind and the tide, at the same time as supporting the incredible weight of the sodden carpet and its precious cargo. It was no good. They simply hadn't the strength.

Surely, Fate would not be so cruel as to allow them to come this far and then fail in their mission? And yet, it seemed that, indeed, they would have to abandon their efforts if they themselves were to survive... They had no strength left and their Admiral shook his head sadly as he realised his brilliant rescue plan was going to fail at the last minute.

Winnie felt his heart sink in his chest even more quickly than it had lifted two minutes before. Those angry tears started pricking at his eyes again but then, as if an invisible power were rising up within him, he spoke to himself very sternly: 'I am a co-pilot! And what do co-pilots do when their captain is indisposed? – they take charge! And I am also a gentleman! And I am surrounded by three ladies who are in a terrible state of agitation – Hissie, Sylvester and Myrtle Turtle! And what do gentlemen do when they are in a situation like that? They reassure the ladies! And, besides, I'm not alone – Plug is here!'

And then he found himself once again speaking in a very grown-up and manly voice:

'Don't you distress yourself, Miss Myrtle! Where there's a will there's a way! We are all SO grateful to you and your magnificent armada for giving us, the Malekidi Moggies, a second chance! You have all done a wonderful job today and, without your courage and help, I wouldn't be speaking now. I'd be at the bottom of the sea... Rest assured that Mr Plug and I will come up with something...!'

Myrtle Turtle looked up at him gratefully, and so did the Admiral; and Hissie and Sylvester smiled weakly with hope in their eyes which were still stinging terribly from all that salty water. And Plug beamed with pride at his young friend.

But all the beaming and smiling didn't make any difference – they were still stuck out there in the middle of the sea, miles from land, with the waterlogged carpet in danger of sinking, and a dangerously injured Loulou on board...

Hissie was still muttering, 'I am a warrior, not a worrier, and Sylvester was still planning how she would be able to teach her to swim in double quick time. She knew that Plug and Winnie got swimming practice when they were away at sea but poor Hissie hadn't a clue. Meanwhile, Plug was tugging at his whiskers in a thoughtful sort of way, and Winnie was trying not to let it show that his brain was in a complete scramble.

And then, just when they thought things couldn't possibly get any worse, the blue sky began to go dark – *really* dark. Surely they weren't going to have to face a thunderstorm on top of everything else?! But, yes, a massive black cloud was sweeping in from the west and already it had almost obliterated the bright sun.

Meanwhile, even though they knew they couldn't actually haul the carpet to shore, the turtles were still struggling bravely to keep it afloat until somebody could come up with a rescue plan. But they really were in the last stages of exhaustion and so the Malekidi Moggies kept finding themselves within a whisker of the terrifying darkness of the deep water all over again.

And with every passing moment, the sky was getting darker and darker until suddenly – BOOM! – the whole world shook as a voice, louder and more powerful than any of them had heard before, or could even have imagined, thundered all around them, from the North, the South, the East and the West, as well as below and above them:

'The Lords of the Earth and Sky have summoned us this day!' thundered the disembodied voice. 'The word has gone forth to the farthermost corners of the universe, "Derrashah is in mortal danger! The great and mighty Derrashah requires assistance! Derrashah MUST be saved!" And so WE ARE HERE!'

And as the terrified moggies looked up into the blackening sky, they saw an amazing sight:

'Those aren't thunderclouds!' Winnie gasped. 'They're... they're *dragons*...! Huge, enormous DRAGONS!'

'Yes!' Came the booming voice. 'We are the dragons of the Mesaoria Plain and we have risen up to save the most important moggy on the entire planet – the one and only Mighty Derrashah...'

'So those hills *were* sleeping dragons!' Winnie whispered under his breath. 'Loulou was right! Oh, I'm such a twit, I'm such an idiot!'

And then, out loud, he started to speak: 'I'm so sorry, Mr... er... Sir...' (how *did* you address a dragon? Your Lizardiness? Your Dragonship? Your Reptilian Excellency?)

'No need for formalities at a moment of crisis!' boomed the voice of the leading dragon. 'It's actually 'Your Scaliness' but you can call me Cyril. And the rest of my crew are Cecil, Septimus, Surtees, and Sid,' he added, indicating the other four dragons now hovering over the carpet. 'We'll have you shifted in no time and then these poor turtles can rest and recover from their heroic efforts. We'll re-launch you into the sky, see you safely home, and then the rest will be up to you...'

The surge of relief that washed through them was so massive it was almost like being knocked over by a huge wave and being half drowned all over again (except in a nice way, if you can imagine that). But then yet another awful truth dawned on Winnie:

'Oh, Cyril, Sir,' he blurted out, 'Loulou – I mean Derrashah – is still very ill and the carpet won't take instructions from me so, once you've got us airborne again, we'll be back where we started – with an out-of-control carpet and our beloved Loulou at death's door...'

'Do you honestly think the Lords of the Earth and Sky hadn't thought of *that*?!' Cyril boomed back, belching out a cloud of green smoke. 'The whole purpose of rousing us from our home on the Mesaoria Plain was to rescue the great Derrashah! Trust me and try to be patient!'

And, in perfect unison, Cyril, Cecil, Septimus, Surtees, and Sid swooped down and plunged their enormous talons all around the edge of the carpet. 'Right, lads, HEAVE!' shouted Cyril, and they spread their leathery wings and raised the carpet up into the air as if it were as light as a feather. And as the four moggies peered over the edge, still clinging to the motionless Loulou, they saw all the hundreds of turtles bob back up to the surface of the sea, their faces red from exertion. What heroes!

'OK!' boomed Cyril again, as the carpet levelled off. 'Let's get this carpet DRY!' And, before any of the moggies realised what was happening, the dragons had all breathed out in unison, engulfing them in hot smoky air which smelt pleasantly of lavender and which miraculously and instantaneously removed every droplet of water from every thread of the carpet and from every tiny hair on the moggies' coats. It felt so wonderful to be dry again that Hissie didn't even worry for a moment about the fact that her fur was now so fluffy that she looked like a puffball.

They were alive! They were dry! The carpet was dry! And they were being towed by five enormous dragons! They were now floating so smoothly that it was hard to imagine that only a few minutes before they had been facing turmoil and almost certain Death.

'All right you lot,' Cyril announced, addressing the moggies, 'it's time for the most important part of our mission. And, Winnie my lad, you're about to meet an old friend! Now, first of all, I want all four of you to join hands in a circle around Derrashah – whom I will now refer to as Loulou because that is how you know him best.'

They did as they were told and Hissie found herself holding on very tightly with one paw in Winnie's and the other in Plug's. She was shaking like a leaf as she looked across to where Sylvester was also clutching the two gentlemen's paws. Sylvester winked at her encouragingly but still she shook. However much of a warrior she was trying to be, it had all been more than she could really stand. Even though they were safe, she couldn't quite rid herself of the awful terror she had been feeling ever since Loulou had been so badly injured during his efforts to save that big snuzzle aeroplane.

But now something new and equally strange caught her attention. What was this *new* apparition? As the four of them sat, staring at Loulou's battered form, a golden mist began to appear all around him so they could no longer see clearly what was happening. Winnie was the first to begin to be able to make out something – or someone – beginning to take shape beside Loulou's head, but who or what it was he couldn't say. They all peered intently as the shape within the mist began to solidify. And then, yes, Winnie could see that it *was* an old friend! He was unmistakable! It was the old mystical Indian cat, Mog Dahl!

Winnie felt his heart glow within him as the wise old moggy turned his smouldering amber eyes in his direction for a moment and smiled a secret smile before turning all his attention to the pitiful sight of Loulou's immobile form.

Winnie was *certain* that Mog Dahl would be able to perform a miracle – especially after his magical advice had popped into Winnie's mind just a few days ago, enabling him to hypnotise his old foe the blunt-nosed viper at the Monastery of the Cats. Mog Dahl could do *anything*!

Everything seemed very quiet and still as Mog Dahl placed his right forepaw on Loulou's heart and held his left forepaw up to the heavens. Then he began to sway gently from side to side, humming to himself, 'Mmmm, Mmmmm, Mmmmm...' Over the next two minutes, the hum began to get louder and louder until it seemed to be coming from

every part of Mog Dahl's body, making him vibrate all over like a huge Harley-Davidson motorbike revving up. And then – *CRACK!* – a bolt of lightning shot out of the sky and into Mog Dahl's outstretched paw. The Malekidi Moggies looked on in amazement as the crackling electricity travelled all the way along Mog Dahl's arm, through his chest and then along the other arm – *ZAP!* – into Loulou's heart, where it flashed bright blue and sent dazzling flashes of flame all around Loulou's body until his whiskers were sending out sparks and his tail began to twitch.

All this time, Mog Dahl had continued to vibrate and hum 'Mmmmm, Mmmmm, Mmmmm...' but now he became silent and bowed with great reverence over Loulou's face. He paused for a moment and then took one enormous breath and breathed it out directly into Loulou's black nose.

Just one breath was all it took...

Loulou's green eyes opened wide, the bandages round his head dissolved, revealing that no wounds remained. He gave one huge stretch, sat up, and grinned from ear to ear as his gaze fell, first, on Mog Dahl and then on Winnie, Hissie, Sylvester and Plug.

Loulou was back! And not only was he back but he looked healthier and younger than he had ever looked before – and happier too. Oh, SO happy!

It was all too much for Hissie. The stress and strain, the ups and downs of the day had finally brought her to her knees and she collapsed into Plug's arms, sobbing her heart out with a mixture of relief and grief and happiness and excitement and tiredness, all jumbled up together.

And so it was that the first thing Loulou saw as he sat up, his big green eyes shining with new life, was something that took them all completely by surprise...

As Hissie's shoulders gradually stopped heaving up and down and her weeping subsided, Plug gently wiped a tear from her cheek with his big gingery paw and said:

'I'm a man of few words, my dear Hissie, so I won't make a fancy speech, but all this drama and all this danger has made me decide I don't want to waste a single minute of this precious life.' He paused for a moment and swallowed hard before continuing. 'I've so enjoyed the times we have spent together, my dear... And... And... Well, do you think you would ever consider making me the happiest old sea-mog in the world...? Hissie, beautiful, fluffy Hissie, will you marry me?'

It was as if the whole world were holding its breath. Up there, in the soft orangey rays of the setting sun, there was complete silence. The dragons were gliding noiselessly on the air currents, not even needing to flap their great wings let alone cough out any smoke. There was no sound at all, just a huge, echoing silence. And Winnie, Sylvester and Loulou himself were sitting as still and as silent as statues, all eyes turned on Hissie. Plug's face was anxious and Winnie saw him gulp and noticed that he was trembling.

When Hissie spoke, her voice sounded very frail, in fact she could hardly speak at all:

'Oh my dear, dear Mr Plug – I do so want to say Yes, truly I do. I... I... have grown to love and admire you *very* much but...' and now she started to sob all over again, '... you see, I couldn't bear to leave my Malekidi friends, I just couldn't bear it – especially after thinking that we had lost our beloved Loulou today... Oh, I'm so, *so* sorry...' And she crumpled again on to the carpet and Winnie felt his own heart might break as he saw the crestfallen expression on Plug's face.

'Now, now! What's all this about leaving your friends?!' It was Loulou's voice. 'Mr Plug is one of US! He IS a Malekidi Moggy! Dear Hissie, you won't have to leave Number 9 Malekidi Street just because you're going to marry Mr Plug – because, yes, you ARE going to marry him! Mr Plug will simply join us in Malekidi Street – if he would like to, that is...'

By way of reply, Plug beamed and nodded his head vigorously and clasped Hissie's paw.

'So that's all settled, then!' said Loulou. 'We'll make a cosy little flat for you at the far end of the veranda so you can have your own home but you'll you'll still be part of the Malekidi family.'

'Oh yes... Well, of course... If we can all be together, I would *love* to marry you Mr Plug!'

Up th
of th

189

Whereupon Plug gave her an enormous hug and said:

'Thank you, oh, thank you! – and thank *you*, dear wise magical Loulou! I can guarantee you will always be well supplied with fish when I'm away at sea – I'll send Walter with a big basket of sardines and shrimps every couple of days... Truly, I must be the happiest moggy on the planet!'

'No!' interrupted Hissie, who had quite recovered by now. '*I am!*'

'No!' insisted Winnie. '*I am!*'

'No!' Loulou and Sylvester chimed in together. '*We are!*'

And they all laughed and laughed at the same time as shedding a few tears of pure joy. Loulou was safely returned to them; Hissie and Plug would be married and the whole family would be together; Sylvester hadn't had to teach Hissie how to swim; and the dragons of the Mesaoria Plain had saved the day! Even Winnie had to pinch himself to make sure he wasn't dreaming.

Oh, what light hearts the Malekidi Moggies had as Cyril, Cecil, Septimus, Surtees and Sid finally brought them within sight of their journey's end. Night was falling as the dragons unhooked their talons from the carpet's edge.

'We have fulfilled our mission,' thundered Cyril, 'and we wish you all the best of the best of the best. The Lords of the Earth and Sky will forever protect you... Captain Loulou is once again in full command and control. We bid you Farewell!' And with a final great *Whoosh*, the five mighty beasts disappeared into the night, returning once again to rest in their green and grassy disguises, as silent hills upon the Mesaoria Plain.

And no sooner had they vanished from view than Loulou took a deep breath and spoke to the little group before him:

'This is a joyous night indeed! In a few minutes we shall once again be home after what must be the longest day any of us can remember! We must have lived more drama and adventure in the last 12 hours than most creatures experience in a full year!

'But before I give the carpet the command to land, there is something I must say and do...'

Plug and Hissie, Winnie and Sylvester pricked up their ears and fixed their eyes on their dear friend, who was now standing tall and looking down lovingly at them as they sat at his feet.

'The first thing I must do is APOLOGISE...' And he raised his paw for silence as they all started to interrupt and try to contradict him. Winnie was saying that Loulou couldn't possibly have anything to apologise for... And Hissie was trying to say that he was the greatest cat that had ever lived... And Plug and Sylvester were simply shaking their heads in disbelief.

But, No, Loulou was adamant:

'Please let me speak,' he said firmly, his paw still raised. 'I DO have something to apologise for and it is important that you allow me to explain: it is *entirely* my fault that you have all been put in such fear and danger today... A Captain must take responsibility when he is in charge and this is what I am doing now. I'm taking responsibility and apologising. You see, in my rush and hurry to rescue the snuzzle aeroplane this morning, I permitted myself to make an almost fatal error. I left the carpet without first handing over responsibility to my co-pilot – young Winnie here. If I had followed the guidelines properly and handed over as I should have done, the carpet would immediately have started taking instructions from Winnie and all this drama would have been avoided... We would have been back in Limassol in less than an hour and I know that you would have taken me straight to Big Mamma at The Cat's Whiskers, because she knows all the best doctors in the neighbourhood. But instead, a massive rescue operation had to be set in motion by our wonderful turtle friends, and then the Lords of the Earth and Sky had to send the Dragons of the Mesaoria Plain to complete the mission. All because of my failure to do what I should have done...'

He paused and smiled down at the four long faces around him:

'Don't be sad!' he said. 'I know that you all think I'm something really special...'

'But you *are!*' they cried in unison before he could say another word. 'You're Derrashah – the Lords of the Earth and Sky agree with us! You're the most important moggy on the planet!'

'All right, all right!' Loulou laughed. 'I admit I do have a lot of clout BUT it is for that very reason that I am making this important apology. Sometimes those of us in high positions make mistakes – nobody's perfect... And when we do, it is much better that we stand up and admit it...

'But this is leading up to something even more important that I want to say to you all before we land: while I was out cold, I was still able to watch you and listen to you and I'm deeply touched by the love and care you showed me. But more than touched, I was so PROUD of you all. You did magnificently and I'm honoured to have you as my friends and family. AND,' he added, turning to Winnie, 'you, young man, have proved yourself a worthy co-pilot. You kept your head, you tried to comfort Hissie and Sylvester, you were very, very brave...'

Winnie squirmed with pleasure as the others looked at him, nodding their heads and smiling.

'And so,' Loulou continued, 'I am bestowing on you with immediate effect the Order of Co-pilot First Class, which means that, if ever anything like this happens again, which I sincerely hope it does not, you will *automatically* assume control and the carpet will turn to you for instructions and will obey you instantly and an unfailingly.'

And he touched Winnie's cap with his paw and immediately magicked a double silver star on the peak, and an extra band of gold-and-silver braid appeared all around the rim.

'And finally,' Loulou said, 'there are a couple of reasons I'm actually extremely *pleased* I made my great error... The first is that, without all this drama, I'm fairly certain that Mr Plug would not have felt emboldened to ask our beloved Hissie for her paw in marriage...' – at which words Plug and Hissie blushed crimson while Winnie and Sylvester cheered – '... And the second reason I'm pleased about my mistake is that, without all the drama and that stupendous rescue, the scene below us would never have happened either... Come along all of you – take a look over the edge!'

What a sight met their eyes!

Now that night had fallen, all around the carpet was pitch darkness, but the street below was blazing with light – clouds of fireflies, strings of glowworms, dozens of catnip lanterns, and hundreds of shining eyes from hundreds of cheering moggies.

And there wasn't a snuzzle in sight!

It was hard to understand what was happening down there. Winnie, Hissie and Sylvester were filled with a mixture of excitement and confusion (*Why* were there no snuzzles?)

They could hear the Malekidi Monsters banging on their dustbin lids for all they were worth and, as the carpet began to descend, they could make out individual faces in the crowd.

'There's Big Mamma!' exclaimed Winnie in delight. 'And look, Loulou – there's your cousin, Mr MacFurrson!'

'Goodness me, so it is!' said Loulou with a laugh. 'He must have got the night off and come down to celebrate our safe return! How quickly news travels!'

By now, Winnie was pointing out some of the nice young lady-cats to Hissie and Sylvester, and Plug was thrilled to see that a whole bunch of the harbour cats had come along as well:

'I can see Hing Fing Ping down there!' he shouted in Winnie's ear. 'Oh, and Hong, Fong and Pong as well!'

'Yes!' Winnie shouted back, above the noise of the Malekidi Monsters' drumming and the hoots and cheers from the crowd. 'And I can smell those delicious spicy fish heads they always cook! My mouth's watering!'

'Mine too! And I bet they've brought their Chinese Checkers and Miaow Jong game as well... And I'm sure the Malekidi Monsters will let you join in later with your flute – it'll be what snuzzles call a jam session!'

'Sounds good to me!' Winnie said, thrilled to discover that his precious flute was still on the carpet despite all the drama.

Plug put his arm around Hissie's shoulders: 'There's my sister, Molly!' he exclaimed. 'She'll be SO happy to hear about our engagement, my dear!' And Hissie blushed and smiled and wiped away a tear. And Sylvester put her arm around Hissie's shoulders too and they all cuddled up together trying to take in everything that was going on below.

The closer the carpet got to the ground, the more they could see and smell, and the louder the noise became until it was almost deafening.

Winnie could hardly believe his eyes. 'Even Hercules, the king rat, is there!' he yelled. 'And Gloria his girlfriend! I hope she's brought some of that lovely catnip champagne!'

'Oh, I'm sure she has!' Loulou said with a chuckle. 'We aren't going to be short of food or drink tonight! I can even see Plug's old friend Mr Tomasaki from Japan and he is bound to have brought along some of his special fish-and-seaweed treats!'

'And there'll be plenty of entertainment too!' Plug chipped in. 'Look over there: our muscly Russian friends from the dock have set up their wrestling ring and are

challenging young dudes to have a go! And no doubt Winnie will be able to show off his limbo dancing again! '

Now it was Hissie's turn to speak: 'Oh, and look over there! Walter has got *Chloe* in his basket! He must've been to pick her up from Valerie Snuzzle's balcony!' And she waved wildly, jumping up and down, until she caught Chloe's eye and they beamed at each other.

'I could see the whole thing from my balcony!' Chloe called. 'I've been so *worried* all day! But then Walter came and gave me the good news – and here I am!'

And scampering in and out between all the dancing moggy paws were thousands and thousands of rats and mice and lizards and insects of every kind, all in their best party clothes and best party mood.

But best of all was the fact that, far from feeling knocked about and exhausted from their adventures of the day, the Malekidi Moggies all felt WONDERFUL. Every single one of them felt as good as new – as if they had had a good night's sleep instead of the terrifying day which had just come to a close. They had no aches, no pains, no cuts, no bruises, no collywobbles of any kind.

As the carpet landed, gently depositing them back on dear old Malekidi Street, with the crowd around them all clapping and cheering, they felt better than they had ever felt before.

Only Loulou knew that this final miracle, this sudden complete restoration of their health and strength, was the loving work of the Lords of the Earth and Sky – and their mystical messenger, Mog Dahl, who was still floating around, half solid moggy and half mist.

'Thank you, Great Ones,' Loulou whispered into the night air. 'Thank you, O Great and Merciful Ones!'

And, in response, a gentle breeze arose around the carpet – a breeze with the fragrance of fresh grass and roses and the salty sea, and Loulou knew his prayer of gratitude had been heard.

Malekidi Street had never seen such a street party as there was that night! And the reason that the moggies had the whole place to themselves so they could celebrate in style was because all the snuzzles were locked inside their houses watching an extra long news programme. The main story was about a hijacking which had taken place over Limassol that very morning and which had apparently been foiled when an enormous black cat had appeared on the nose of the aeroplane. The snuzzles were glued to their television screens for hours as the pilot told the story, and then the passengers were all interviewed and then all sorts of so-called Experts came on to talk about what *they* thought had really happened, and whether that huge black cat was real or not...

But the Malekidi Moggies and their friends had better things to do than watch the News. Under the starry Cyprus sky, they laughed and sang and hugged each other, and danced the night away.

THE
END
maybe...
9
197

APPENDIX

Let's take a closer look at a few of the illustrations:

Pages 6-7
Here we see nine – or is it ten? – moggies snoozing in Katie Snuzzle's magical mystical garden. And if you look closely, you can see loquats and pomegranates, ripe and ready to eat.

Pages 26-27
This picture shows the Malekidi Moggies setting off on their first magic carpet ride. From left to right we've got Sylvester, Hissie with her picnic basket, Winnie in his smart new co-pilot's cap, and Loulou. On the far left you can see some of the Limassol skyline – and if you flip back to the Contents page, you'll see Number 9 Malekidi Street where it all began.

Pages 40-41
This is Shipwreck Bay. You can see the wreck sticking up out of the water and the Malekidi Moggies sailing overhead – this time with Plug aboard. The turtles are coming up on to the shore to lay their eggs and they have very distinctive tracks which you can see in the sand. Cyprus has two kinds of turtle: the green turtle and the loggerhead. Our friend Myrtle Turtle is a green. There are plenty of moggies out there in the sand dunes and you can also see the strong currents in the water which make it very dangerous for swimming and which almost swept poor Myrtle to her death.

Pages 50-51

Welcome to the Cat's Whiskers Club! And, yes, that's a real mouseburger in Winnie's paw, complete with tail sticking out (that's the best bit)...

Page 66

Here's the beautiful fishing boat, The Courageous Sea Cat. It has a very special moggy-pennant as well as a map of Cyprus at the top of the main sail. And those big eyes which you can see painted on to the prow of the boat are for protection and can be found on a lot of Cypriot boats. You can also see Walter the chief seagull at the top of the mast and you will also find Hercules the giant rat, as well as Plug enjoying some off-duty time, stretched out in the sun.

Pages 114-115

If you go to Limassol Castle, you'll be able to see just about everything in this picture – everything except for Chloe and Winnie and the three crooks at the back, that is. The suit of armour, the pot, and the carving of the leopard, are all there, just as they are in the painting.

Pages 120-121

Here we see Richard the Lionheart, wielding his battle axe and fighting with all his might amongst the Limassol sand dunes. His shield bears the magnificent red and gold coat of arms of England. The red crosses on the English soldiers' tunics and the horse's caparison mark them out as Crusaders. Further behind are the blue banners of Isaac's men.

Pages 132-133

These are the kinds of brightly coloured clothes which wealthy people in the Middle Ages wore to special occasions like Richard the Lionheart's wedding to Berengaria. And the dance music was provided by minstrels playing mediaeval instruments such as the different kinds of flute you can see here.

Page 155

Old Nicosia Airport is a strange place indeed, frozen in time. It was one of the most exciting places Winnie could imagine – silent and spooky and no snuzzles about. Here in the picture you can see the Cyprus Airways jet which was the very last passenger plane to fly into Nicosia before the snuzzle war of 1974.

Pages 156-157

From high up here we've got a great view of lots of the places we've been to in Hissie's Happy Holiday, including the ancient Roman theatre of Curium, Lady's Mile Beach, and the Monastery of St Nicholas of the Cats, along with a couple of other famous places which aren't actually mentioned in the story – the Salt Lake with its flamingos and the ruins of ancient Amathus. And can you see the sleeping Dragon...?

Page 161

This fearsome looking creature is a Blunt Nosed Viper, the most venomous snake in Cyprus. It is the one Winnie came across at the Monastery of the Cats – the one he was able to hypnotise with Mog Dahl's Special Stare and whom he then recognised as his old sparring partner from centuries before.

Page 171

The official name for this rather strange looking moggy is *Felis Silvestris Lybica*. It is the most ancient kind of domestic cat ever discovered and is the one which Loulou talks about when the Malekidi Moggies are flying over Shillourokambos just before they spot the hijacked aeroplane.